D0115175

THE PENDULUM'S TRUTH

LEIGH BROWN & VICTORIA CORLISS

~Titles by Brown Corliss Books~

Second Chances

The Pie Sisters

The Pendulum's Truth

This is a work of fiction. Names, characters, places, and incidents either are the product of the authors' imaginations or are used fictitiously, and any resemblance to actual persons, living or dead, business establishments, events, or locales is entirely coincidental.

Copyright © 2018 Leigh Brown & Victoria Corliss

All rights reserved.

ISBN-13: 978-0-692-13779-6

To Life's Journey:

May we all navigate your peaks and valleys

with grace, appreciation, and infinite gratitude.

Acknowledgements

The Pendulum's Truth was inspired by countless stories from family, friends, and strangers, all of whom provided the threads in what would become the fabric of our novel. Thank you to those that shared their testimonies of how serendipity and faith touched your lives.

Thank you to Mary who spent many hours teaching us how to develop a deeper and more meaningful spirituality. You showed us how to recognize the signs and to interpret what they mean. Your connection to the universe and your willingness to embrace everything that comes your way was an inspiration.

Thank you to Liz for introducing us to the pendulum and its powers. Your understanding of chakras, auras, and energy expertly piloted us through a new spiritual world; your unflagging support and encouragement moved us to "get it right."

Thank you to Jennifer. Your wisdom, guidance, and "aha" moments while commuting, helped us bring our characters to life and tell a better story.

To Lesley, our editor. With skilled precision, you critically shaped The Pendulum's Truth into best form by dotting the i's, crossing the t's and so much more. Thank you for your dedication and quiet perseverance.

As always, thank you to our families. Your unwavering

support as we brought The Pendulum's Truth to life was a blessing. We are forever grateful that each and every one of you is a part of our life journeys.

The Pendulum's Truth

CHAPTER 1

Everything happens for a reason.

Ava could feel Mary's breath brushing up against her ear as she whispered the words. Goose bumps prickled both her arms and she briskly rubbed them away. It would be just like her mother to reach out to her so soon from the other side, to reassure her daughter that everything would be all right. Mary's words were not surprising; it was a mantra that her mom had lived by for as long as Ava could remember. Now, staring at Mary's pale face and vacant eyes, Ava was comforted knowing that she had no regrets. They had been on a journey together as her mother battled cancer and Ava had been there every step of the way.

Hours earlier, the nurses had called. It was time, they said. Grabbing a tote bag, Ava had quickly filled it with essentials: the files that contained her mother's medical records and legal documents, a water bottle and a few magazines to bide her time. Once she had what she needed, she had jumped in her car and driven to Riverwoods Memorial Hospital. Although she had been expecting the nurse's call, it still unnerved her to think the end was finally here. She wanted to tell her mother she loved her and let her know that it was okay to let go of this life. Ava hoped the right words would come to her.

Pulling into the parking lot thirty minutes later, she found a space close to the entrance and hurried inside. Ava nodded to the receptionist behind the front desk and made her way to the elevators, nearly knocking over a young woman holding a wrapped sandwich and a bottle of iced tea.

"Oh my goodness, Sara. I'm so sorry. I didn't see you." Ava fumbled as she grabbed the young woman by the elbow.

The nurse looked up as she steadied herself. "Ava! Don't worry about it. I was just getting some lunch to take back to the floor. I'm so sorry to hear about your mother. She was a special lady, such a fighter right until the end."

Ava's heart clenched. "What do you mean? Am I too late? I hurried as fast as I could."

Sara smiled uncomfortably, confirming her fear. "I'm not sure," she said, backpedaling. "I left a little while ago. Let's

2

go see what's happening." She gestured to the opened elevator doors. When they reached the third floor, Ava hurried toward her mother's room. Inside, a nurse, wearing pink scrubs and a stethoscope around her neck, stood by the window. She smiled warmly at Ava as she entered. Her mother lay under the covers, looking peaceful, but Ava could tell that she had moved on to another realm.

"I opened it just in time," the nurse said softly, motioning to the window.

Ava nodded, acknowledging the superstition that an opened window before death allowed the soul to escape from the body and enter the next life. "Thank you, Julia. That means a lot to me."

She approached the bed and kissed her mother gently on her forehead, noting that her skin had already cooled. Julia patted her arm and pulled a chair over to the side of the bed for Ava to sit.

"Take your time," she said. "I'll close the door. Just let me know when you're ready."

Julia reached for Ava's hand and squeezed it gently. "I want you to know your mother wasn't alone. I was right here with her when she was ready to go. She's at peace now." With that, she left the room.

Ava turned to her mother. "Oh, Mom," she said quietly, as tears crowded her eyelashes and threatened to fall onto her face. "I'm sorry I didn't get here in time. I love you so much, I hope you know that." It was then she'd heard Mary's whisper.

Everything happens for a reason.

Ava had not always agreed with her mother's thinking. Even now, she wasn't entirely convinced it was true despite the countless conversations, debates really that they had had over the years about fate and destiny.

"Mom," she'd argued, sitting in a beach chair on the hot South Carolina sand of Sully Shores where they had a family cottage. "It's so easy to say everything happens for a reason, because that leaves the ugly parts of life in someone else's hands. I can blame everything that doesn't go my way on the fact that it wasn't meant to be. I don't ever have to be accountable. Is that what you're saying?"

Applying more sunscreen, Mary adjusted her straw hat to shade her eyes. "No, Ava, you're not hearing me. I'm not saying your life isn't yours to live. *You* are in complete control -- your life, your decisions. But at the same time, I believe that life is full of signs; they're everywhere, and you have the ability to recognize them. It's a gift. Maybe it's a coincidence or just an odd feeling you have. You know, those 'aha' moments when you say, 'Oh, now I get it.' Those moments are when we can learn so much about ourselves, if we're open to them."

Mary took a long drink from her water bottle and continued. "And if the signs are confusing, don't be discouraged. Life doesn't always come neatly wrapped in a box with a bow on top. Sometimes we don't know why things happen the way they do, but at the end of the day you just have to embrace it all. It's all part of your journey, Ava."

"Okay, okay. I get it. Look for signs and don't expect life

to always be neat and easy. Is that what you're trying to tell me?" Ava had chuckled as she shifted in her beach chair.

"Laugh all you want," her mom scolded. "But you'll see. The older I get, the more I'm convinced there are other forces at play. You know, your father sends me signs all the time letting me know he's still with me. It's comforting, even after all these years. Just try to keep an open mind, Ava. Promise?"

"Okay, Mom, I promise I'll keep an open mind." Instinctively, she felt for the sea glass pendant resting lightly on her chest. The turquoise sea glass encased in silver wire was a gift from her father. She never took it off.

Years before, when her dad had died unexpectedly, Ava and her mom had clung to each other for comfort, bonded by their shared love and loss. Now Mary was gone, too, and Ava was a team of one. For how long, she wondered? Bending low, Ava clasped her mother's hand, gently stroking the paper-thin skin. "I love you, Mom. What am I going to do without you?" Ava felt a breath pass by her ear again.

"I'm going to send you someone good."

CHAPTER 2

Ava left the hospital, letting her emotions take over as she put the business of arranging for her mother's remains to be transported to the funeral home behind her. Life was so unfair. At thirty-two, she should be thinking of a husband and children, not burying her parent. Perhaps it was selfish to feel that way, but Mary's death was not a surprise. It had been a long time coming and Ava was almost relieved that her mother's painful suffering was over. But her mom's passing also marked the ending of a family, as Ava knew it. She was an only child, with no other relatives to speak of; just her two best friends from college, Georgia and Kassi. "Sisters of the heart" they called themselves.

There would be infinite details to work out. Sadly, she had been down this road before. Although much younger when her dad died, Ava still remembered the chaos surrounding his death. She hadn't been much help to Mary then, but she knew from that experience that there would be endless phone calls to make and papers to sign. Wearily, Ava drove home unsure if like her mother, she was strong enough to handle it all.

Despite her own grief, Mary had always made certain that Ava felt loved and secure. After her husband's death, Mary had resisted the temptation to hover over Ava like a low-flying helicopter. She knew she could not protect her daughter forever or from everything, so when high school ended, as hard as it was for her, she had insisted Ava go away to college.

After much discussion, Ava chose the University of South Carolina; it was away from home, but not too far. Mary stood firm; Ava would live on campus and take full advantage of all the things college life had to offer. There were many nights her freshman year when her homesickness had threatened to derail her, but with the help of her roommate Georgia, a blond beauty from Dixieville, she slowly came into her own.

She loved walking across the campus's historic Horseshoe, appreciating the cool shade cast by its great oaks with their branches that dipped low, almost to the ground. Classes provided an unexpected challenge as she tried to reconcile her professor's expectations with her own; just as she had been warned, college was no place for handholding. Time management was an unfamiliar responsibility and yet there was something oddly freeing about creating your own schedule. She was growing up, little by little, and she was ready.

One warm November evening during her freshman year, Ava and Georgia were lying on their bunk beds, their books propped up on pillows. As Ava swept her yellow highlighter over the text, she pulled the loose strands of her chestnut hair off her face and tucked them behind her ears.

"Hey Georgia, there was a notice in the lobby that the Hospitality Club is looking for volunteers to bake food for homeless shelters. You know, for Thanksgiving? I think I might check it out. It's at Capstone. Do you want to come?" Ava rolled onto her side and stared up at Georgia's bunk.

Georgia hung her head over the edge and peered down at Ava, her blonde hair falling Rapunzel-like towards the floor. "Baking? I don't know. The kitchen isn't my happy place. I usually leave that stuff to my Mom."

"Really? I love it. It's kind of relaxing. Oh come on, it'll be fun. And besides, we'll meet people -- you're the one always saying we have to get out of this dorm more."

"True," agreed Georgia, her big, green eyes squinting as she considered Ava's proposal. "I'll tell you what. I'll go with you, but if it's not my thing, don't be mad, okay?"

Ava smiled. "Deal!"

Two days later, they hurried after classes to the kitchen at Capstone, taking their places on stools as a tall, lanky girl stood before the group of twenty students. She had long, dark hair that was meticulously curled into waves and wore a short, yellow sundress with ruffles, and matching ballerina flats.

"Welcome everyone. My name is Kassi Scott." She spoke loudly so the group could hear her. "Thank you all for coming. We're here to make baked goods for Thanksgiving baskets that will be distributed to homeless shelters in Columbia. We have experienced bakers scattered throughout the room, so pick a table and they'll tell you everything you need to know."

Kassi approached Ava and Georgia. "You two, come with me," she directed. "I'll show you what to do."

She made her way to an empty table, gesturing for the girls to follow her. After exchanging introductions, they tied clean aprons around their waists and washed their hands. "You ready?" Kassi asked as she handed them note cards with recipes for blueberry muffins and Southern cheese biscuits.

"Oh, these sound good," Georgia said as she perused the biscuit recipe. "Just so you know, Kassi, I'm not very handy in the kitchen." Georgia paused as she surveyed the room. "I'm really just here to check out the guys."

Kassi laughed. "Sorry to disappoint you, Georgia, but there aren't any guys here. Not that we haven't tried, but they just don't show up." She shrugged nonchalantly, knowing full well whose loss it was. "They don't know what they're missing."

The next two hours flew by as Ava sifted, stirred, and

baked dozens of blueberry muffins and biscuits. The girls clicked right away, talking incessantly and getting to know each other. Kassi was a sophomore from Charleston, a business major with an eye on a financial career. She had three older brothers and, as the only girl in the family, was her mother's pet project for all things feminine. Ava now understood why Kassi looked so put together. She lived in the Honors dorm in a suite with three other sophomore girls and had briefly flirted with the idea of pledging a sorority but after attending a few pledge parties, she decided the rules of being a sorority sister were not for her. She was more of a free spirit, so she joined several clubs instead--Student Government, Hospitality Committee, and Ultimate Frisbee. Ava wondered if there was anything Kassi couldn't do.

Georgia was raised on her parents' farm in rural Dixieville. She loved riding her horse, Gunsmoke, and had competed in equestrian events throughout the southeast. Her younger sister, Jojo copied everything she did, which was annoying. Although now that she was away at college, Georgia actually missed her sister, sometimes.

"What about you?" Kassi pointed at Ava. "What's your story?"

"Well," Ava hesitated, not wanting to disappoint her overachieving new friend. "I grew up in Laurelwood, so I'm only about an hour away from home. I'm an only child, so there was no one to annoy." Ava laughed. "I'm not sure what I want to major in yet; maybe business or maybe hospitality. I like being with people, but I'm not very comfortable with strangers. I'm not like you, talking to everyone. You act like it's no big deal."

"Are you kidding?" Kassi chortled. "With three older brothers? If I didn't speak up, I would never have been heard!"

"Good point." Ava nodded. "My house was pretty quiet. It's just my mom and me. I was young when my dad died and we've been really close ever since. My mom's the one who pushed me to come here even though I know it was hard for her to see me go, for me too. I miss her a lot."

"You're doing the right thing," Georgia chimed in, supporting her friend. "You're here, working hard and making your mom proud. My mom says I'm lucky to be here. She's always telling me that the next four years will be the best years of my life. You know, because you're on your own, deciding who you want to be but still only a phone call away if you screw up."

Ava smiled at her roommate. "You're right. I'm lucky to be here too."

"Yeah, you are!" Kassi interjected. She handed each of them a muffin, still warm from the oven. "We all are."

CHAPTER 3

"Georgia, I have to get out of this room. My brain is going to explode if I study anymore. Broadmore is such a dick about pop quizzes. One a week? Really? And you never know when they're coming. I knew I should have taken Kincaid, at least she sticks to scheduled tests." Ava jumped off her bed and thrust herself into a deep knee bend, stretching her stiff muscles.

"I warned you. Broadmore is notorious for those quizzes. Karen told me it was her hardest class." Georgia sat straight in her desk chair and pointed accusingly at Ava. "But you didn't want to listen to me."

Scrunching up her face in disgust, Ava admitted, "You're right. But seriously, I need a break." She checked the time on her watch. "It's already seven o'clock. Do you want to go to Russell House, to that event I told you about? We can go check it out and if it sucks, I'll come back and study some more."

Georgia shook her long blonde hair free from a ponytail holder and reached for the makeup mirror sitting on the corner of her desk. "If we go anywhere, I need to fix this face first." She pointed to her flawless skin, gesturing to some imagined imperfection. "What's going on at Russell House again?"

Ava was already standing in front of their small dorm room closet, clothes stuffed into every square inch of it. Now juniors, she and Georgia shared everything; they had stuck together through the highs and lows of freshman and sophomore years and had become inseparable. They were "sisters of the heart," after all.

And just like sisters, they shared a unique bond. But they were different from each other, too. Ava was more serious while Georgia was carefree. Ava took time to think before acting while Georgia moved full steam ahead. Ava was willing to step out of her comfort zone and consider other points of view; Georgia was most comfortable with both feet firmly planted in Georgia Land. It was a perfect combination that made for a great friendship.

"It's called 'Find Your Spirits.' It's a takeoff on Spirit Week. I think they're going to have a psychic comedian and a tarot card reader and some other things." Ava pulled a short denim skirt out of the bowels of the closet and held it up to her waist. "Is this yours or mine?"

Georgia pulled her gaze away from the mirror and looked at the skirt. "Yours," she said definitively. "Just so you know, I will *not* be getting my tarot cards read. People who claim to see into my future scare the shit out of me."

Pulling a red tank top out of the dresser drawer, Ava laughed. "Georgia, honestly? You're such a baby. I'm definitely getting my cards read. I hope the place isn't packed."

Ava changed her clothes and was putting on mascara when her phone rang. "Can you see who that is?"

Georgia leaned over her desk to read the phone screen. "It's Kassi. Want me to answer?"

"Yeah," Ava answered, gliding the mascara wand over her eyelashes with steady precision. "See if she wants to come with us."

"Hey, Kassi," Georgia spoke into the phone. "We're heading over to Russell House. They're having that 'Find Your Spirits' event with the tarot card readers and all that psychic stuff. Want to come with us?"

"Sure," Kassi replied. "I'm bored." Kassi's senior year schedule was easy as pie; she had already lined up a job and was coasting through to graduation.

"We're changing now. Meet us outside our dorm in fifteen minutes."

"You got it," Kassi replied. "See you then."

Thirty minutes later, the three girls stood outside Russell House waiting in a short line. "I hope they have a bar. No one's gonna tell me my deep dark secrets without a drink first. You know what I mean?" Kassi smiled her best "this is horse shit, but I'm sure I'll be amused" smile.

Ava narrowed her eyes at Kassi and Georgia. "Clearly, I'm on my own here. I should have just come by myself." She looked at Georgia. "You're afraid." Pointing at Kassi she said, "And *you're* going to make a mockery of the whole event."

Kassi rolled her eyes. "Whatever."

Once inside, Ava was amazed by all the sights and sounds. Dozens of tables and booths lined the main floor. She quickly scanned the signage and noted tarot card and palm readers and vendors selling everything from crystals and incense to holistic energy drinks. A few hundred students and faculty were browsing the booths. Thankfully for Kassi, a large bar was set up at one end of the room.

"Let's let Ava roam around. Come get a drink with me. I'm buying," Kassi instructed, pulling on Georgia's arm. "We'll catch up with you later."

Relieved to be left on her own, Ava started down the first aisle. She passed a booth selling all kinds of essential oils and incense. She paused briefly and inhaled, taking the scents deep into her lungs. Moving on, she noticed a table with a man behind it displaying hundreds of rocks and crystals. "Create Positive Energy for a Positive Life" a sign read. She smiled at him, but did not stop to talk.

By the time Ava got to the second aisle, she found what she was looking for. On a table covered with a plain white cloth was a sign that read "Let Me Tell You What Lies Ahead." *Why not?* She thought, smiling to herself. What did she have to lose?

"Hi," Ava said as an older woman stood to greet her. She was tall, dressed casually in khaki Bermuda shorts and a blue, short-sleeved blouse; a pair of red readers adorned her head like a hairband. If Ava had not known better, she would have guessed she was on her way to a bridge club or a ladies' lunch.

"Hello," she said, inviting Ava to have a seat. "My name is Carolyn. Have you ever had a reading before?" She waited for Ava to make herself comfortable.

"I'm Ava, and no. This is my first time."

"Great. Let's get started. Hold my hands so I can read your energy." Ava did as she was told. Carolyn closed her eyes and squeezed gently. A current of electricity, moved through her like a live wire that tingled throughout her body. Intrigued, she opened her eyes. There was something extraordinary about the young woman sitting in front of her. "You have a powerful energy about you," she said at last. "It's unusual for someone as young as you. You must feel things very deeply. It's a special kind of intuition, you notice things most people don't."

"What kinds of things?" Ava asked, distracted by the tingling sensation in her hands.

Still stroking Ava's skin, Carolyn answered. "You're able

to make connections, to make sense of things. You understand there are reasons why things happen the way they do. Most people just don't pay attention. But, I think you don't know your own strengths, or maybe you're a little afraid to explore them. Am I right?" She didn't bother waiting for Ava to respond.

"It's up to you to decide if you truly want to learn how to use your gifts. They're yours to develop." Carolyn pulled Ava's hands more tightly into her own. "One more thing. There's someone close to you who has them, too."

Ava thought of her mother, and wished she were here. Mary would not have been a bit surprised by this information, but she was. What were the odds that two people who had never met were both so sure she had untested gifts? Coincidence?

Gently, she pulled her hands away. She needed time to process what Carolyn had said. She just hoped she could remember every word. "Well, thank you for the insight. You've given me a lot to think about."

Carolyn smiled broadly, nodding her head. "You're very welcome. By the way, I knew you were coming to see me today."

Ava smiled politely, playing along." You did?"

She pointed to Ava's neck. "I meditate every morning to let the universe know I'm open to receiving messages. This morning, I saw a beautiful beach, miles and miles of sand. Then I saw sea glass, stacked in blue and green pieces and sparkling in the sun. Your necklace tells me the message was meant for you."

CHAPTER 4

Despite being busy as she settled her mother's estate in Laurelwood, Ava was lonely. All the paperwork and packing she was doing to prepare the house for sale made the time pass, but it was solitary work. It would have been nice to have someone to share it with. The logistics were overwhelming. There were phone calls to be made, and agencies to be notified; every time she had to put a copy of the death certificate in the mail, it hit her all over again.

Georgia visited from Dixieville when she could, but with her husband, Alex, often traveling for business, she was busy caring for their three small daughters. Ava was grateful that she managed to call most evenings after the kids were in their pajamas, watching television and waiting to be tucked into bed.

"How are you holding up?" Georgia asked, sounding exhausted.

Not wanting to burden Georgia with her issues, Ava tried to deflect. "Good. Still lots of loose ends to tie up, and there's more paperwork to go through then I could ever have imagined, but I'm making progress. How about you?"

"Oh you know, same shit, different day. These kids run me ragged, but I love them! Poor Alex, there's so much estrogen running around this house, I don't know how he stands it." Georgia paused, and Ava could hear a little girl's laughter in the background. "Ava, if you need anything, you'll let me know, right?"

"I will, but you have your hands full. I just appreciate your checking in, it means a lot. And when I get everything settled, maybe I'll come for a visit and see the girls. In the meantime, I have to make some decisions about what comes next for me."

"Well, I hope I'm the first to know," Georgia replied. "You can always move to Dixieville. It would be like old times, just the two of us."

Ava laughed. "Funny, I don't picture you the life of the party right now. I don't think you have time or energy for that." She hung up, thankful for her supportive friends.

Kassi stopped by whenever she came through town. Now a successful sales representative for a large pharmaceutical company, she traveled all over South Carolina. Dressing the part in business suits and designer shoes, she carried herself with a confidence that Ava had envied since college.

"How is your leave of absence from Thornton's going?" Kassi asked one day when they met for breakfast. "I bet they've really missed you since you left to take care of your mom."

Ava frowned. "Well, I'm running out of time. They've been great, but understandably they need me to make a decision by the end of the month."

"You mean, whether you're going back or not?"

Ava nodded. "I've been thinking a lot lately that maybe it's time to shake things up and make some changes. Thorton's has been a good to me, but it's just a job. You have a career, Kassi. You love what you do and you're more successful every year. I'm thinking it's time for me to find something I love to do, too. Now, more than ever, I feel like time is precious, and I bet if my mom were here, she'd be the first one to tell me to go for it."

Kassi drew a forkful of scrambled eggs with melted Gouda cheese to her lips and chewed slowly. "I know she would."

Ava shrugged. "So, I have a few crazy ideas, that maybe could work, but right now, I'm still sorting out Mom's affairs. I have to pack all her things and figure out what to do with them, although, I'll probably just store everything at Sully Shores for now. I've decided I'm definitely keeping the cottage. I could never sell it."

"I don't blame you." Kassi was sympathetic, wiping rye toast crumbs from her lips with a napkin. "That cottage meant so much to your parents. Would you ever move there? Get a job in town?"

Ava paused. "I couldn't live there right now. Honestly, I'm afraid to even visit. It'll be like a time capsule. When Mom and I went back after Dad died, it was awful. His moccasins were sitting by the back door and his wallet and keys were on the kitchen counter. The hardest part about losing him were the things he left behind. You're afraid to touch anything because it seems disrespectful. And secretly, you hope that if you leave everything exactly the way it was the day he died, he'll be back for it. Every time I visited, it was like ripping the bandage off a fresh wound. And then one day, I showed up and the shoes were gone and the countertop was cleared and I knew that my mom had begun to heal."

Kassi stood, wrapping her arms around Ava and hugged her. "It's okay. Give yourself some time; it's not going to happen overnight. If you think a change is what you need, you should do it. I'll help you if I can. You just need to decide."

Ava's plan had presented itself a few weeks later, as she settled herself at a table at Sunny's Diner. Enjoying a cup of coffee and a cinnamon roll, she listened to the buzz of activity around her. Nearby, two young mothers ate pecan muffins and shared gossip while their babies slept soundly in carriers at their feet. A few tables away, an elderly couple sipped coffee while they silently perused the local newspaper.

Feeling unusually content, Ava took in the conversations around her. Customers, waitresses and cashiers all bustled about, easily sharing the small space. The vibe was happy and energetic. Ava felt herself relax.

The diner door slammed, switching on the figurative light bulb in her head. *That's it!* She grabbed paper and a pen from her purse, and began scribbling down her thoughts as they came into focus. She had never dreamed of starting her own business, but now, somehow it just felt right. With an open mind, she let her imagination take flight.

Every business course she had ever taken came back to her as she tried to make sense of her notes. It all boiled down to one simple equation: knowledge + expertise + passion = success.

That said, there was really only one type of business Ava would consider; a small bakery or a coffee shop. She had the passion part of it down; ever since college and baking muffins for the Thanksgiving baskets. She had also joined the Hospitality Committee, catered student events, and did a work-study program for The Breakfast Bar, a campus morning hangout. In fact, any activity that involved baking or cooking was her cup of tea. But any thoughts of turning her culinary interests into a lucrative career were purely daydreams. Ever practical, Ava had chosen to earn a degree in finance instead.

Now, that business degree would come in handy. She wanted to stay close to Sully Shores. At the same time, it was important to find somewhere new; where memories of her parents did not crowd her thoughts. Ava worked on her business plan, fine-tuning the details. Kassi scrutinized it as well and then showed it to an attorney friend for a professional seal of approval. After the legal considerations were resolved and she had financial input from a local bank, Ava felt like she was finally ready to move forward.

The first step was to find a property. She wanted a small town with a strong sense of community that she could call home. She scoured real estate magazines and online sites looking for the perfect place. There were several towns, not too far away, that would fit the bill. Moreland seemed like a good possibility for setting down roots; although it was surrounded by several similar towns, that might also work.

One afternoon Kassi called, just as Ava had finished prioritizing her real estate needs. "Hey! How are you doing? I'm on my way to Hilton Head. I know I'm not supposed to talk and drive, but I'm blue-toothing, so don't yell at me."

"Hilton Head? What's up there?" Ava asked, organizing her papers into a dog-eared manila folder.

"I'm going for a business retreat. You know, schmoozing and all that." Kassi breezily replied.

"Well, if anyone can schmooze, it's you." Ava chuckled.

"Don't sell yourself short. You've come a long way from freshman year. You know, if you open a coffee place, you're going to have to schmooze, too. Your customers are your lifeline. You are your own brand!"

"Yes, I know," Ava replied, a hint of nervousness

creeping into her voice. "It's slightly terrifying to think I'll be responsible for an entire business. What if it doesn't work?"

"Oh, you'll be fine." Ava imagined Kassi swatting the air to indicate it was no big deal. "You understand business, which is a huge step in the right direction. And we all know that you're a master in the kitchen, so I know people will love your product. When do you start looking at property?"

"Tomorrow. I'm heading to Moreland to meet a realtor. Wish me luck."

"Hey, embrace it all, the entire experience, and make sure you send me pictures. Okay, gotta go." Before Ava could respond, Kassi had disconnected.

CHAPTER 5

The next day, Ava pulled into a parking spot in front of a small diner in Moreland. She was scheduled to meet with a real estate agent whose name she had found in one of the flyers. In fact, each time Ava found a listing that looked interesting the same agent's name had popped up: Charlotte Boyer. When she called her, Ava had liked the sound of her voice. It was friendly, but professional. She hung up the phone with a sense that she was in good hands.

Early for her appointment, Ava went inside the diner. She grabbed a menu and a small table in front of a large window facing the street, the better to people watch while she ate. A young girl with a brunette ponytail and big, silver hoop earrings took her order, a pulled pork sandwich with a side of peach slaw and a sweet tea, and headed back to the kitchen. Ava spread the newest real estate flyer in front of her and stared at the commercial properties. Moreland, Huntsville, and Wicks Falls were all small towns with charming main streets. It might be difficult to find something that had room for a storefront and an additional area for her to live, but working and living in the same space was a priority. She wanted to be completely connected to her work.

The young waitress returned, depositing Ava's food in front of her. "Can I get y'all anything else?" she asked, reaching into her apron pocket for a straw and some extra napkins.

"I think I'm good. Thank you though." The waitress smiled and moved on to another table.

Starving, Ava dug a fork into the sandwich. The shredded pork, soaked in a spicy barbeque sauce, melted in her mouth. The peach slaw was crisp and tangy, with cabbage coated in mayonnaise with a hint of honey. She opened the small bag of potato chips and spilled the contents onto her plate. The crispy chips were the perfect contrast to the creamy slaw.

Just as Ava was finishing her lunch, the front door opened, ushering in a gust of warm air and a middle-aged woman she could only describe as ethereal. She was average height with a huge head of curly red hair, a ginger Medusa. The afternoon sunlight peaked through the sheer layers of her gauzy gold dress. She scanned the restaurant quickly, her profile showing off a prominent nose almost too big for her face, before making eye contact with Ava.

She walked over to Ava's table. "You're Ava Dell," she said with a warm smile.

"I am. Are you Charlotte?"

Charlotte's curls bounced as she nodded and extended an arm stacked with beaded bracelets, each a different jewel tone color. Their hands touched in greeting, sending a jolt through Ava like an electrical charge. Startled, she tried to pull her hand away, but Charlotte's firm grip only grew tighter. She stared fixedly at Ava.

"Yes, I'm Charlotte Boyer. It's nice to meet you." With a final squeeze to Ava's hand, she pointed to the open flyer on the table. "Are you already looking at properties already? I love it when clients are prepared."

"I was just taking a peek. This came out yesterday. You got my email with all of my specifications and budget, right?"

Charlotte nodded and Ava continued. "Please, sit down. Are you hungry? Do you want me to grab a waitress for you?"

Taking a seat next to Ava, Charlotte busied herself arranging the many folds of her dress beneath her. "It's okay. I have a drink coming. I'm here so often the girls know to bring a glass of iced lemonade when they see me."

"Nice!" Ava smiled broadly. "That's exactly what I'm looking for! And that's why a small coffee shop makes so much sense for me. If I can find a space that supports twenty to twenty- five seats, I should do great. But, just as important,

I want to be part of a town that supports its local businesses; a sense of community is really important to me."

"I understand. Do you have a specific location in mind? Any of the towns around here would welcome you."

"I'm open. I'd prefer a small town, but one big enough to support my business obviously. And if I can find a space that includes an apartment for me to live in as well, that would be ideal. I'm sure I'll be working long hours trying to get things going."

Ava hesitated. "I hope you don't think I'm strange, but I'm also looking for a place with really good energy. I want people to come and hang out; so I can get to know them, just like they know you here." Small pools of tears gathered in the corners of Ava's eyes catching her off guard.

Charlotte reached over, covering Ava's hand with her own. Again, Ava's skin tingled. "What's the matter, Honey?" Charlotte asked softly.

"I'm sorry. My mother passed away earlier this year and she would be the first person to tell me to pick a place that really spoke to me. She, of all people, would appreciate the importance of good energy." Ava dabbed her eyes dry with the sleeve of her blouse.

Charlotte gave Ava a long look. "I'm sorry to hear about your mother. Were you close?"

Folding her hands in her lap, Ava took a moment to control her emotions. "Very. My dad passed away when I was much younger, so it was just the two of us for a long time. A few years ago, she was diagnosed with cancer. She fought so hard. She didn't want me to be alone, but life doesn't always work out the way you want it to, I guess."

Charlotte pushed her red curls back from her face, her beaded bracelets clinking together. "Losing a parent is awful. Losing both parents by your age must be…" Charlotte paused, looking for the right words. "Well, it must be devastating."

"Look at me, sitting here crying like a baby," Ava mocked herself. "And I wanted today to be all about new beginnings."

"It's okay." Charlotte smiled, waving off Ava's apology. "I understand what you mean about wanting to make your customers happy. I can tell you this. You have to love people to be in the service industry. Look at me. I deal with people all day long. By the time I find a client the right house or property, we're practically family. It's really about knowing how to connect with people."

Ava stared at Charlotte.

"Call me crazy," she chuckled, "but I think things happen the way they're supposed to. I can't even tell you the number of times that deals fall through and buyers are crushed. I hear it all the time, 'I'll never find anything as perfect as this.' And sure enough, a few weeks later I get a phone call and the same buyers have found their *real* dream home and it's even better than the one they lost out on. I could have told them the first house wasn't right, but they never want to hear it."

"How do you know that?"

"I feel it in my bones." Charlotte smiled.

"Like a hunch?"

She was coy. "I'd call it something stronger than that."

"You mean like intuition?" Ava asked, thinking back to her reading with Carolyn at Russell House.

"Sure, intuition is a nice way to describe it. Some people are more intuitive than others. I put myself in that category," Charlotte paused. "Intuition? Knowing signs when you see them and understanding them? Whatever you choose to call it, it certainly has helped me to navigate through life."

Ava knew all about signs. "My mother used to say that they were life's little coincidences."

Charlotte looked at Ava, intrigued. "Your mother knew what she was talking about. I happen to think the universe is full of signs. You just need to know where to look for them. The naysayers would say that it was all hocus pocus and ridiculous. I guess it depends on whether or not you believe we're guided by a higher power."

"My mother believed that she had a sixth sense. She described it as knowing when things were coming, and she was convinced that I had it too. I mean, I guess sometimes I felt that way. When I was in college, there was a woman who gave me a reading. She told me I had the same gifts as my mother, but who knows? My mother always told me just to keep an open mind."

Charlotte nodded her head. "You have to keep an open mind and be receptive. If you are a person with those kinds of gifts, you need to. . . ."

A woman wearing a t-shirt that read "Fabulous and Fifty" and cropped denim pants approached the table with a tall glass and a white plate.

"Hi ya, Charlotte. I've got your lemonade. I thought you might like some fresh praline bars, too. They just came out of the oven a few minutes ago."

"You know I'll never turn down one of your famous praline bars. Thank you, Christine. Ava's going to love them, too."

She gestured to her tablemate. "Christine, this is Ava Dell. She's looking to open a new coffee shop around here."

Christine smiled beseechingly at Ava. "It's nice to meet you, but please don't set up shop in Moreland. We like to think we're the best place here to get a cup of coffee and...well, a praline bar." Christine held up the plate of cookies.

Ava laughed, taking a homemade cookie from the plate and placing it on a napkin. "Point taken. I wouldn't want to encroach on your customers. I love the atmosphere here though. It's exactly what I'm hoping to create for myself."

"Where are you looking?" Christine set the glass of lemonade in front of Charlotte.

"Well, I'm trying to find a small town with a busy main street. I need good foot traffic and easy parking. I was just looking at a few options." She patted the real estate magazine in front of her.

"So I see! Wicks Falls is nice. My niece Mary Jane lives there and loves it; they have a town center and main street just like we do. I can't think of any coffee shops in town. I know they have one of those franchised coffee places. And there's Joey's, but that's more of a luncheonette."

Ava turned to Charlotte. "What do you think of Wicks Falls? Do you think I could find what I'm looking for there?"

"That's where my office is, so I know the town very well." Charlotte thought about it for a minute.

"There are a few properties that might have potential. There's a storefront on Blanche Street that could work. It's not exactly on the main road but it intersects with it. There's an office condo on Hanna Circle. But that's not on the first floor, so maybe it's not an option."

She pulled an iPad out of a very large leather tote and consulted the MLS. "Wait a minute, there's another place. It's a small two-story house on Palm Street in the center of town. Let me just check one thing here. . .yes! It's zoned for mixed use. That means you can use it for both commercial and residential purposes. The first floor has about 1,000 square feet. The second floor has about 850 square feet, the perfect size for a one-bedroom apartment with a separate entrance outside the building. It will be cozy, but cozy is good!"

Ava's eyes lit up. "How much is it, Charlotte?"

Charlotte stared intently as she scrolled the tablet screen.

"Well, I know it's been on the market for a few weeks. It's in a good area on Palm Street, lots of visibility. There's a small public parking lot behind the building next to it, and there's additional street parking in front. The first floor used to be a tailor's shop. I know there is a kitchen that you can probably work with and a first floor bathroom for customers."

"It sounds perfect! But can I afford it?" Ava asked impatiently.

"Well, the list price is definitely within your budget. I know the agent well. I'll call him and ask if there's any wiggle room. That way you might have some extra money for improvements and decorating. If we can get in this week to look around, are you available?"

"Anytime this week would be perfect. I'll make myself available."

CHAPTER 6

Nervous energy propelled Ava through the purple door of the Sweet Carolina Real Estate agency, her excitement growing with every strappy-sandaled step. Once inside, she took a moment to regroup, self-consciously smoothing the crisp pleats of her white cotton dress. "Today's the day," she promised herself. "A new beginning. A fresh start. No tears today."

"Good morning!" Charlotte greeted her as she clasped Ava's hands in hers. She tipped her chin towards the clock ticking on the wall. "You're right on time."

Ava's skin grew hot at Charlotte's touch. She wondered

if Charlotte noticed, but the realtor was already walking back to her office. "Come with me," she summoned. "I found a few more places to show you in addition to the one we talked about yesterday. It's always good to have options."

Charlotte's long stride moved her swiftly down the hall away from Ava, her hair waving like a red flag behind her. Ava hesitated. She was standing on the edge of a huge opportunity, but if ever there was a time to proceed with caution, this was it. Charlotte's green skirt floated around her ankles capturing Ava's attention, and beckoning to her as Charlotte disappeared into her office. Ava's lips twitched upward. Taking a giant leap of faith, she hastened after Charlotte.

She plopped into a chair in front of Charlotte's desk. "I did some research online last night, and liked everything I read about Wicks Falls."

"That it's a mid-size city with a small-town feel? That it's big enough to support commercial business, but small enough to be a real community? That the only thing better than visiting Wicks Falls is living here? That. . . ."

"Yes! Yes! Yes! All that and more!" Ava interrupted Charlotte's spiel, pulling a manila folder from her purse. She shuffled briefly through the pages inside before selecting one in particular. "I printed out all this information last night. Wicks Falls is everything you just said and more."

Scrolling her finger down the page, she read, "Real estate taxes are affordable, fire taxes are reasonable, the school system is among the top ten in the state." She placed the sheet on top of the desk, and recited the rest of her list from memory.

"I love the hometown feel of the old fashioned ice cream parlor and the bandstand concerts on the common. The library is so beautiful, architecturally elegant." She opened her arms wide. "The whole town is just so quaint, even the post office."

Built in the 1800s, the Civil War-era building was iconic in its stature, the grandeur of its ornate façade like a stone watchdog looming protectively over the picturesque streets of Wicks Falls.

"Well, it certainly sounds like Wicks Falls has everything," Charlotte agreed.

"Almost everything," Ava qualified.

"What's missing?"

"I'm pretty sure it doesn't have anything like The Tea Cozy. That's the name of my new place," Ava announced proudly. "What do you think?"

"The Tea Cozy." Charlotte savored the name. "I thought you were opening a coffee shop."

"Tea and coffee, but the pastries will be the real draw: muffins, scones, croissants, and cookies baked fresh every day."

"I like it," Charlotte declared. "And, there's definitely nothing else like it in town."

"Fantastic!" Ava was eager to get started. She stuffed the manila folder back into her purse and jumped to her feet.

"So, can we go now?"

Hours later, a full day of viewing properties drew to a close as Charlotte parked her car in front of a narrow, two-story wooden building. Nestled in a cozy row of colorful pastel storefronts, the pale yellow structure needed no introduction.

"I saved the best for last," Charlotte explained. "You like?"

"It's perfect. "

Ava was mesmerized as she studied the place from top to bottom. Two windows stood sentry to the second floor, where just as Charlotte had said, there was a small apartment big enough for one and as close to work as you could get. Even sight unseen, Ava already knew she loved it. At street level, two more large-paned windows, with a sky blue door sandwiched between them, welcomed in the afternoon sunshine and passersby. Of course, the building was empty right now, but that would change soon enough. She glanced at the brass numbers centered above the front door.

"716 Palm Street." She read the address aloud. "Well, that settles it," she said decisively.

"The address?" Charlotte raised an amused brow.

"Yes. No. Well, all of it really. Everything is perfect, the building and the location. It really feels like a neighborhood even though it's a busy main street. The fact that 7 and 16 are my lucky numbers is an added bonus. There's not a doubt in my mind; this was meant to be."

From her vantage point in the driver's seat, Charlotte studied Ava's profile and nodded shrewdly. "Clearly you know something about astrological meanings and sun signs. So do I."

Ava grinned, pleased that Charlotte understood. "A little bit. My mother loved the astrological signs. I'm an Aries; Mom always said that explained my creative side, but my emotional tendencies she blamed on my dad. He was a big softie when it came to me. Every sign also has its lucky numbers; mine are 7 and 16. When they're combined like 716, that's really special; it can mean a big change or a new beginning lies ahead." Ava gazed adoringly at the building. "And I need both."

"Maybe you're right," Charlotte agreed. "Let's take a look inside just to be sure." She pulled a key from her purse. "Ready?"

The two women entered the sun-infused building, Charlotte turning on lights as they moved beyond the yellow rays' reach, to the back of the room. "This used to be a tailor shop," Charlotte explained, making her way into a small kitchenette. "An older couple, Eddie and Myrtle Hayworth, rented the space and fashioned it to meet their needs. Eddie took all the measurements, while Myrtle did most of the alterations. And every day, she made lunch for both of them in here."

Ava explored the room with its sink, stove, small refrigerator, and section of built-in shelves. More than likely, Myrtle had used them to store her canned goods and spices.

"All the utility hook-ups for a working kitchen are

already in place," Charlotte noted, "but obviously, it will need some remodeling and renovations for your purposes."

Ava nodded, taking a final slow turn around before moving again to the front room. A spacious square, it would easily hold several 2- and 4-person tables. She pictured a room full of patrons, business people grabbing a cup of coffee and a muffin before work; girlfriends stopping in after the gym or tennis for a refreshing iced tea and a light lunch; mothers with babies sleeping in their strollers looking for a quiet haven to enjoy a beverage and a snack.

"I see it, too." Charlotte stood beside Ava surveying the empty room. Spreading her hands in front of her, she painted a picture. "The Tea Cozy, whether you need a morning boost, or an afternoon pick-me-up."

Ava closed her eyes, imagining it. "If I do this right, it will be amazing, but I'll tell you a secret," she said to Charlotte, her eyes still glued shut. "I'm scared out of my mind."

Charlotte patted her shoulder reassuringly. "Let's go look upstairs."

It took no time at all to check out the small apartment. "No chance of getting lost in here," Ava laughed.

"Too small?" Charlotte worried.

"Not at all," Ava assured her. "I love it. It's like my own little sanctuary." Charlotte was visibly relieved.

"There's something about this place." Ava waved her hands indicating where they were and beyond. "Wicks Falls, too. I think I'm in love."

Charlotte laughed and looked at her watch. "It's only 4:30. If you're sure this is the place, I can get to work right away making it yours."

"I'm sure."

With a broad smile, Charlotte hugged Ava, giving her shoulders a friendly squeeze. "Welcome home, Ava."

That evening, Ava sent pictures to Georgia and Kassi wanting her friends to share in her excitement. This was a huge moment. Ava could finally put the past behind her and move on.

Moments later, Georgia squealed with excitement on the phone. "Ava, I love it!"

"I do, too!"

"I love the big windows and all the natural light," Georgia added.

Ava agreed. "Yep. It's gonna be perfect. I just know it."

CHAPTER 7

With thumb and forefinger, Ava rubbed the sea glass pendant like a worry stone; a single bead of sweat trickled down the back of her neck. A sleeveless pink linen shift and silver sandals invited the cool touch of the air conditioner, but her heavy chestnut mane hung loose to her shoulders, covering her neck like a warm winter scarf. With one swift motion, she twisted it into a loose bun, breathing a sigh of relief as the chilled air caressed the skin of her neck.

She glanced at Charlotte seated to her left, calm, cool, and collected in her usual attire of chiffon and sheer. Those now familiar scarlet tresses danced in time to the trademark bands of beaded bracelets dangling from her wrists. Clearly this was not her first rodeo, a fact Ava found comforting as she took stock of the others in the room with them. There were seven of them total gathered around the polished wood conference table for the closing; Ava, her attorney, and Charlotte; the seller, Mr. Keenan, his realtor, and his lawyer, and a third party escrow agent, Booker Malloy. Booker, Charlotte explained, would lead Ava and the seller through the transaction. The whole process would take about an hour to complete. Eyeing two giant stacks of papers on the table in front of Booker, Ava wondered if an hour would be enough time. She had a ton of signing ahead of her.

"Good morning!" Booker greeted the group, nodding at each of them as they responded in kind. "Well, this is an exciting day for you, Ms. Dell. And I'd guess a bittersweet one for you, Mr. Keenan." Respectfully, he dipped his head to the gentleman seated across from Ava. Seventy-something Jack Keenan had been a real estate mogul in Wicks Falls for decades. When he and his wife decided to move closer to their son and his young family in Florida, they quickly began selling all of their real estate holdings, until only their own home and 716 Palm Street remained.

"Definitely some mixed emotions going on today." Jack cleared his throat, sitting a little straighter in his chair. "But it's time for my next adventure." He turned to Ava and smiled. "My wife and I love Wicks Falls. I hope you'll be very happy here, too."

A lump grew in Ava's throat. "Thank you, Mr. Keenan, I'm sure I will be."

"Well then, let's start, shall we?" Booker pulled the

stacks within reach. "Is everyone ready?"

Ava signed the endless stream of papers Booker placed in front of her, explaining each one as he did. "Don't be afraid to ask questions. That's what I'm here for."

Ava nodded numbly. Who knew closings were so involved? She reminded herself of what lay ahead and knew it was worth every minute. Renewed energy coursed through her fingers as she raced for the finish line, signing the last few papers.

"Now what?" she asked, placing her pen down and looking around the table.

"Now you get these." Mr. Keenan smiled broadly as he handed her two sets of keys, one for the apartment, and one for the space below it. "Congratulations!"

"Thank you, thank you." Ava expressed her gratitude to all of them, turning to face a beaming Charlotte. "Thank you, most of all. None of this would be happening if it weren't for you."

She stood, motioning for Ava to join her. "Come on. It's time to celebrate. Lunch is on me."

Ava and Charlotte said their good-byes, shaking hands with Booker Malloy and the attorneys until they were standing in front of Jack Keenan. "Thank you, Mr. Keenan," Ava said, grasping his hands tightly in hers. "I'll take good care of the place. I promise."

"I know you will." He squeezed her hands gently. "Take care of yourself, too."

"I will." Ava waved to him as she and Charlotte made their way out the door to the Pinkney Creek Tavern and a celebratory lunch.

Lunch at the Tavern was long, leisurely, and delicious. "How about some dessert?" the waitress offered when they had finished their meals.

"I'm stuffed," Ava groaned. "One more bite, and I'll explode."

"You only had a salad," Charlotte pooh-poohed.

"It was an entire vegetable garden with a bushel of crab meat on top of it."

"We have homemade pecan pie a la mode, and a flourless chocolate torte that's decadent," the waitress tempted. "Or my personal favorite, the warm peach cobbler with fresh whipped cream. It's to die for."

Ava licked her lips. "Okay, fine I'll have the cobbler. But if I explode, it will be your fault," she wagged a warning finger at Charlotte. "I'd like a cup of hot tea too, please." She patted her stomach gently.

The waitress laughed. "One tea and one cobbler coming up. Anything for you, ma'am?" she asked Charlotte.

"Just a coffee please, with milk not cream."

She waited for the waitress to leave, while quietly observing her lunch companion. Relaxed in her chair with a full belly and a happy heart, Ava reminded her of the Cheshire Cat.

"You're looking very pleased with yourself," Charlotte noted.

"I am," Ava answered without hesitation. "Six months ago, I didn't know if I'd ever be happy again, but today, I'm a business owner, an entrepreneur, and a first-time homeowner. If my mom were here, she'd say everything happens for a reason, and I think she's right; I highly doubt any of this would have happened if things had stayed the way they were."

"No doubt about it, "Charlotte agreed with her. "You came, you saw, and you conquered. You're invincible."

She looked at Ava with great appreciation. Charlotte remembered being in Ava's shoes, making big life changes that took courage and more than a bit of luck. Now Ava was poised to start her own business and create a new home; Charlotte couldn't be happier for her. She liked this young woman and her tenacity, and imagined that they would become great friends.

But it was more than that; it was the electric charge that had passed between them when they first shook hands. Yes, Charlotte had felt it too, and she knew exactly what it meant. Only once before had she felt such electricity from her hand to another's and she had known instantly that Ava was special. That day they had talked about gifts; just like her, Charlotte knew Ava had them, and now she wanted to show the younger woman her true potential. The moment had come. Reaching into her purse, Charlotte pulled out a box and handed it to Ava.

"What's this?" Ava looked at Charlotte in surprise. The

4" x 4" square of crushed red velvet lined with silver trim felt plush in her hands.

"It's a gift. A housewarming gift from me to you."

Ava stared at the box, itching to open it. *Shit, I didn't get her anything.* With a twinge of guilty pleasure, she lifted the lid.

A silver chain snaked its way through soft folds of ivory satin. A small cluster of colorful and miniature stones gathered at one end of the chain, a pale rose crystal with cream colored veins streaming through it hung from the other; between the two stretched a rainbow of seven minute beads. The quartz crystal was spherical in shape, no more than two and a half inches long, it was thickest at the top, an inch and a half at its widest.

She lifted the object out of the box, holding it by the chain, and raised the pendant to eye level. Ever so slightly, the sphere swung back and forth and then stopped, stilling itself in mid-air. Ava cupped it in the palm of her hand. It was solid, but not heavy. She stroked the pale surface with her thumb and marveled at its smoothness.

"What is it?" she breathed.

"It's a pendulum."

"It's beautiful," Ava murmured, unable to take her eyes off of it.

"It is," Charlotte agreed. "And very special, like you. That's why I want you to have it."

Dragging her gaze away from the pendulum, Ava looked

at Charlotte. "I've never seen anything like this before."

"I'm glad you like it. I have one too, but it's different from yours," Charlotte said. "May I?" She took the chain from Ava to show her what she meant.

"Each of these small beads represents a trait or a strength that you possess," she said, pointing to the miniature rainbow in her grasp and the dangling sphere. "So when you seek guidance from the pendulum, it actually draws power from you to do so."

Ava shifted in her seat, confused. "Seek guidance? What for?"

Charlotte smiled, handing the pendulum back to Ava. "Sorry, I'm getting a little ahead of myself."

The waitress returned with dessert and coffee. They waited quietly as she arranged the cups and plates in front of them, Ava staring at the pendulum, Charlotte watching Ava.

"Thanks. We're all set," she assured the waitress. The coffee was hot as Charlotte sipped it, studying Ava over her cup. Returning it to its saucer, she let the coffee cool as she spoke.

"Do you know the difference between atheist and agnostic?" she asked Ava.

"Not really," Ava shook her head. "I think agnostic means you don't believe that God or gods exist. Atheists don't really know if gods exist. Something like that."

"Basically," Charlotte nodded. "It's an ongoing debate:

belief versus knowledge. Some people can't believe in something unless they can see it. But others, well for us it's our belief that gets us through life. Fate or free will? Like we talked about before, I believe that there's no such thing as coincidence." Charlotte looked at Ava as though sizing her up.

"You remind me of my mother," Ava said. "I think she would have really liked you and I know she would have loved this conversation. Will you tell me more about the pendulum?"

"I'd love to." Charlotte settled into her chair, taking a sip of water to clear her throat.

"To the untrained eye, a pendulum is simply a string or a chain with a pointed crystal, like this one, at the bottom of it." She pointed to the quartz sphere resting in Ava's hand. "It's called a bob. But historically pendulums have been used in lots of ways by many different cultures for thousands of years. Some say Moses even used one to discover hidden water."

She sipped from her glass as if the mere mention of water had made her thirsty. After a moment, she continued. "The pendulum's mystique is legendary," Charlotte said. "It's an instrument of great wisdom with the ability to provide 'yes' and 'no' answers to any question you ask it, big or small. Questions provide guidance or affirmation."

"As the spiritual owner," she pointed at Ava, "*you* work with the pendulum, asking questions and interpreting the answers. I use my mine every day, like a personal advisor. I ask it things I need to know for work, for my private life, or for whatever is most important to me that day."

"That sounds easy enough." Ava spoke slowly, watching the quartz crystal spin on its silver chain. "Ask questions and get the answers."

"You got it," Charlotte told her. "Sometimes the pendulum tells you what you don't want to hear, and that can be really hard to accept."

Well, that doesn't sound good. Ava carefully returned the pendulum to its nest. She closed the lid, and discreetly placed it in her purse.

"One last thing," Charlotte added. "There's a small booklet underneath the lining. It will help get you started on your pendulum journey. Study it and do what it says, verbatim."

A nervous smile tugged at Ava's lips. She believed in many different things, but the pendulum was a bit out there, even for her. On the other hand, she had promised her mother she would keep an open mind. No time like the present.

"Thanks, Charlotte. I'm not sure I'm the right person for this, but I'll give it my best shot."

"You'll do fine." Charlotte crossed her arms leaning back in her chair. "Remember when we met and shook hands? I know you sensed it too. I've only felt that kind of energy once before when I first learned of my own gifts, but I didn't have someone to explain it all to me. If I can do that for you, or rather, if the pendulum can, then your life will truly be full."

Charlotte gave her an encouraging smile. "And don't worry, I'm here to help, any time. You know where to find me."

Still not certain if Charlotte was right to gift the pendulum her, Ava raised her spoon to her mouth. "Good cobbler."

CHAPTER 8

A few weeks later, on a seasonably warm Wednesday, Ava's phone rang. Spring in South Carolina was often hot and sticky, and today, Wicks Falls was no exception. She pulled the phone out of her back pocket, checking the screen.

"Hi Charlotte! I've been thinking about you. How's your day going?"

"Pretty good, thanks for asking. I'm actually calling to see how everything is progressing. Oh, and to let you know that all the paperwork for The Tea Cozy has been officially recorded at City Hall. I told you it usually takes a couple of weeks for everything to be finalized. Well, it's done. There's no going back now."

"That's great news! I know I made the right decision."

"Well, you sound very confident," Charlotte chuckled. "Like someone who's been using her pendulum perhaps?"

Ava was apologetic. "I'm sorry. I've been so busy getting the shop ready I haven't had any time to look at it. Trust me, I want to, but by the end of the day, I'm just too tired. There's still so much to do here."

"I understand. You're probably swimming in sawdust from all that construction. No worries, there's no timetable. Look at it when you get the chance. And remember, I'm here to help anytime."

"I know. You've been more than wonderful, especially these past few weeks. I can't thank you enough for all of your recommendations and referrals. And yes, it's a bit of a war zone here with all of the changes, but I've been pretty lucky so far. No disasters yet, knock on wood," Ava laughed. "I promise I'll look at it tonight."

Charlotte heard a crash in the background. "Uh oh, looks like I spoke too soon," Ava said. "Clay just knocked over the saw horses with his ladder. I've got to go."

Later that day, she climbed the stairs to her apartment. It was still a work in progress. There had not been much to move in, just a few sentimental pieces that had belonged to her mother: an ornately carved dresser with a built-in jewelry box, an arm chair covered in magnolia flowered fabric that Ava remembered as a fixture from her childhood, and a mahogany hope chest with a hummingbird painted on the top, an engagement gift from her father to her mother. The rest of her family belongings would stay at Sully Shores. She completed her furnishings with basics from Davenport's Decor located on the southern end of Palm Street; a simple bedroom set, a small dining table, a couch, and a few accent pieces. It was enough for now. The priority was getting The Tea Cozy ready.

The tiny kitchen boasted full-sized appliances, but tonight Ava limited herself to the toaster oven. She pulled sliced cheese, butter, and a tomato out of the refrigerator. She grabbed a slice of wheat bread from an old-fashioned breadbox and put together an open-faced grilled cheese sandwich. After placing the sandwich in the toaster, she watched as the cheese began to melt and turn golden.

She polished off the sandwich, along with a few handfuls of potato chips in between bites, and recalled her conversation with Charlotte. Charlotte was right; she needed to figure the pendulum out. It was not something to be afraid of, there would be no genie set free, no poltergeist that would jump out and scare her. The pendulum was supposed to help her, and bring clarity to her life.

In the small coat closet next to the front door, a stack of boxes waited to be unpacked. Ava lifted the top box and placed it on a small coffee table in front of her couch. She loosened one of the folded cardboard flaps to reveal the contents. Sitting on top of several tissue-wrapped objects was the red velvet box. Exhaling slowly, she reached in and pulled it from the top.

"There you are."

She placed the box on the table. The cover lifted off easily and Ava placed it next to her on the couch. Reaching inside, her hand touched the smooth coolness of the bob. Gently, she took it out, raised it to eye level, and jiggled the chain. The pendulum swayed slightly then stopped.

Turning her attention back to the box, Ava continued her inspection. Just as Charlotte had indicated, there were some items tucked beneath the layer of heavy satin. She lifted out three small incense packets tied with tiny blue ribbons. Passing each packet under her nose, she inhaled their individual scents before placing them on the table.

Next, she removed two colored crystals; one purple and one a brownish-gray color. She recognized the purple crystal as an amethyst but wasn't sure about the other one. Placing them next to the incense, she took a small silver edged booklet from the bottom of the box. The booklet was no more than ten pages and consisted mainly of drawings and definitions. The script was beautiful, a style of calligraphy that gave an Old English appearance to the words. There were a couple of pages devoted to chakras and a few others explaining auras. The last pages specifically addressed how to get answers from the pendulum.

The pendulum is a very powerful tool, but it is not a predictor of the future. The future is very fluid and nothing is certain. The pendulum is used for truth and guidance. Using it makes you a facilitator. In order for answers to be provided, you must cleanse the energy around you and stay positive.

You must ask the pendulum questions in order to get clarity. For some, it moves left to right. For others, it moves front to back. One direction signifies "yes" and the other direction, "no."

Hold the pendulum by the chain with one hand. Naturally, your hand might make it move. But with practice, you will understand when the pendulum is moving to answer your question.

Each of the seven stones in the chain represents a chakra of the body. The chakras are there to help you align your mind, body, and spirit. There are seven bodily chakras; root, sacral, solar plexus, heart, throat, 3rd eye, and crown. It is important to channel these chakras to find a deeper understanding of self and understand the energy each represents.

Auras gauge the body's energy field. Colors vary from red, to yellow to black. Auras show the condition of someone's spiritual and emotional well being. It's important to cleanse your aura to keep your own energy positive. Energy can be exchanged between people passing close to you. Another person's energy can be absorbed by your own, whether positive or negative.

Start with a prayer. Hold the pendulum chest high to align with your heart chakra before you ask a question. Make *sure your question is small and specific. Frame your question with "All things considered is ......optimal?" or "I'm putting it out to the universe, is ......optimal?"*

If the pendulum does not move, perhaps you are not meant to get an answer at this time."

Ava closed the booklet and sat back on the couch, still cupping the pendulum in her hand. Raising it in line with her heart, she said, barely above a whisper, "Okay. Let's try this. All things considered, is moving to Wicks Falls the optimal thing for me to do?"

She held her hand steady trying hard not to cause any movement. Nothing. The pendulum hung motionless from the chain. She tried again. "I'm putting it out to the universe, should I start my life in Wicks Falls?"

The pendulum held fast. No movement. Ava scoffed at it. "Well, clearly I'm not doing this right." What did Charlotte tell her? *"You and the pendulum work as a team. The pendulum draws its power from you."*

Ava closed her eyes. In her mind, waves broke gently on the white sands of Sully Shores. Seagulls called to each other overhead. The sun warmed the back of her neck as she dipped her toes in the water. Warmth. Peace. Calm. Breathe in. Breathe out. Breathe in. Breathe out.

She raised the pendulum to her heart again and stared at it. This time she focused on the seven small stones in the chain. "Okay, chakras, guide me. Help me to understand. Help me to find answers." She took a deep breath as if to blow out the candles on a cake and exhaled slowly, "I'm putting it out to the universe. Am I meant to be in Wicks Falls right now?"

She stared intently at the pink quartz. The pendulum began to swing ever so slightly to the left. Ava made sure her hand was as steady as she could hold it. No, it was definitely swinging, maybe just an inch.

Yes.

Ava's eyebrows rose with surprise. "Well I'll be damned."

CHAPTER 9

The next few weeks were a whirlwind as Ava focused on the shop below. Workers swarmed to erase the traces of the tailor shop and redefine the space as The Tea Cozy. The interior walls were sheet rocked and ready to paint and the floors were laid with Southern Yellow Pine. Bronze pendants hung from the ceiling every six feet sending soft beams of light to the room below. Today, a painter stood before one of the two glass windows flanking the front door. He was applying gold painted letters that spelled out "The Tea Cozy." The other window would boast "Comfort and Conversation."

"Where do you want this self-serve bar?" John Dixon,

the general contractor asked Ava. "If we put it over to the left of the customer counter then people can easily reach the napkins and utensils after they pay for their order."

John took a tape measure from his tool belt and pulled the end out about an arm's length. "We have just about four, maybe five feet here to build it out." He turned to look for Ava's reaction.

"Yes. That's exactly what I want. Do you think that's enough table space for everything?"

"Should be," he replied, motioning to another worker. "Clay, let's start mapping out the self- serve bar. Here let me show you." He turned away from Ava.

Ava looked around, smiling as she noted the progress. Charlotte's referrals were invaluable, especially since Ava did not know very many people yet. The best name on the list, by far, was John. He really understood her vision for the shop. It was John who suggested installing wide comfortable bench seats below the two bay windows.

"Well, if it was me and I wanted people to stay, I would include some cushioned seating where a person can relax with a book or maybe a newspaper. Add a small table in front of each bay and you've got a couple of real cozy spots for your customers."

Ava loved the idea. The window seats would become the focal point of the shop. She ordered plush cushions and several brightly colored pillows. John built storage beneath for supplies. Ava thought she might keep some children's toys in one seat for mothers in need of distractions for their kids.

Another week and the shop should be finished. Ava had confirmed this morning that the tables and chairs would be delivered in a few days. John had recommended McQuaid's, a commercial restaurant supply warehouse in Moreland, for the rest of the items she needed. There were so many things to order. Paul at McQuaid's had helped her compile a lengthy but complete list of everything from equipment to paper goods and more.

Everyone was so helpful. Ironically, Ava did not need the pendulum to tell her that Wicks Falls was the right place for her to put down roots. There was a hometown charm that drew her in and held her close. People here genuinely cared about each other and she couldn't wait to be a part of it.

Working diligently on her marketing campaign, Ava heard the front door open. She looked up catching sight of Kassi looking exceptionally tall in four-inch pumps, a tan pencil skirt and cream blouse. A large, gold pendant hung from her neck and matching bracelets clinked on her wrists as she entered The Tea Cozy. A pair of designer sunglasses pushed her dark hair off of her lightly bronzed face.

"Kassi!" Ava shrieked, startling the crew. "What are you doing here?"

"Hiya, Ava." Kassi grinned. "I'm here to check out the new place. I was just over in Huntsville meeting with some doctors and thought I'd take a side trip to see what all the fuss is about."

Leaping over a small pile of construction debris, Ava

raced to hug her friend. She stopped just short of an embrace. "Oh, no. I'm filthy. I don't want to get you dirty." She grabbed Kassi's hands pulling her in for an air kiss. "I can't believe you're here! Let me show you around."

Their quick tour of the main floor and kitchen brought Ava and Kassi to two scruffy plastic chairs situated away from the construction noise. Ava quickly wiped the seats free of sawdust and motioned to her friend. "Sit! I'm dying to hear what you think."

Kassi sat, crossing her tanned legs and grinned. "Ava, it's perfect. I love your vision; it's really sweet. It's exactly the kind of place I like to stop between appointments to get something to eat, or check my phone and send a few emails. You've got Wi-Fi, right?"

"Of course! Even I know the world is attached to their smart phones and computers. It's completely wired for the Internet. See those beautiful window seats? My contractor John built them for me from scratch. I have amazing fabric for the cushions with little teapots and teacups on it," Ava gushed.

"Wait! In case you think I've gone overboard, I have to tell you something." Ava leaned closer for emphasis. "You know how terrified I've been to start my own business, but Kassi, the closer I get to opening, the more I have this feeling. I can't explain it except that the energy here is so good and I feel so happy. I haven't felt like this in years."

"That's great." Kassi was thrilled for her.

"This was absolutely the right move for me. And

something else, I met someone." Now she really had her friend's full attention.

"Not that kind of someone," she laughed. "Actually, she's my real estate agent, Charlotte Boyer. She's a little quirky and a lot to take in when you first meet her, but we clicked right away. She reminds me of my mom."

"How so?" Kassi wondered.

Ava grabbed her arm. "She knew things about me without me even saying a word. And after I closed on The Tea Cozy, she gave me something she said I was meant to have."

"And what was that, a bill for her services?" Kassi laughed at her own joke.

"No." Ava ignored her friend's attempt at humor. "It's a pendulum. It's supposed to bring guidance and direction to my life. I just have to figure out how to use it first."

"You're kidding," Kassi deadpanned.

"Want to see it? Do you have a few minutes to come upstairs, and I'll show you my apartment, too?" Ava started out of her chair.

"Hell, yes," Kassi answered. "This I've got to see."

CHAPTER 10

Ava pulled her keys out of her pocket, and unlocked the apartment door to let Kassi inside. A gust of cool air from the air conditioner greeted them as they entered.

"It's not very big, but it's the perfect size for me. I don't plan to be here much," she explained. "The Tea Cozy is going to take all of my time, at least in the beginning."

Kassi looked around. "I love it," she declared. "And I see you brought some things from your mom's house, too, to make it homey. It really is everything you need, Ava, and convenient like you said. Traveling every day for work can be a pain in the ass sometimes. You've got a great commute."

"Exactly!" Ava agreed. "Have a seat on the couch and I'll grab the pendulum."

Kassi sat on the blue chambray-covered sofa and pulled her phone from her tote bag. "Take your time. I'm just going to check my messages and make sure no one is looking for me. Yesterday, I had more than fifty emails just in the time it took me to get home from the office. Honestly, there's nowhere to hide from these people." She ran her fingers through her long hair and twisted it into a bun, securing it with a barrette that she grabbed from the top of her tote.

Ava returned minutes later with the red velvet box in hand. Placing it on the coffee table in front of Kassi, she lifted the cover and gently pulled out the pendulum.

"Here it is," she declared, dangling the pendulum in front of Kassi's eyes. The pink quartz sphere twitched from side to side before falling still.

"Interesting," Kassi said. "What does it do?"

"Well, it's a process really," she replied, oversimplifying things for her friend. First, I have to clear my mind to help me focus. Then, I ask questions of the pendulum, and it answers me."

Kassi moved to the edge of the couch. "Let's try it. What kind of question can I ask?"

"Well I'm still learning how it works, so…" Ava's voice trailed off.

"Nonsense," Kassi asserted. "Ask the pendulum if I'm going to get a promotion. I've been working like a dog and rumor is there are two open spots on the sales management team. If I could get one of them, there'd be a lot less traveling and maybe I could actually start having a life of my own."

Ava sat on the floor with a sigh. She was hardly an expert yet, and having an audience was unnerving, but she did not want to disappoint her friend. Clearing her mind, she focused only on Kassi's question, and raised the pendulum to eye level.

She started with a prayer then asked, "I'm putting it out to the universe. Will Kassi get promoted?" She held her breath waiting for the pendulum to move. Nothing. She tried again. "Do you know if Kassi will get a promotion?" The pendulum held fast.

Kassi's skeptical face said everything; she thought the pendulum was a joke. Ava was embarrassed. She grabbed her phone from the kitchen table and called Charlotte.

"Hi. I think this thing's broken. It's not answering any of my questions today."

"Ava?" Road noise made it difficult for Charlotte to hear her clearly. "What are you talking about?"

"The pendulum. I have a friend here at my apartment and I was trying to ask some questions. Nothing's happening, not even the slightest movement. I just don't get it."

"Hold on, I'm driving. Let me pull over." A minute later, Charlotte continued. "Okay, I'm back. Are you lining it up with your heart?"

"Yes," Ava replied. "I'm holding it right at eye level so

that it lines up with my heart chakra."

"Good. Did you start with a prayer? Are you making the questions very explicit?"

"Yes. Yes! Prayers and specific questions and everything else, but the pendulum isn't moving." Charlotte could hear the irritation in Ava's voice.

"Did you put your question out to the universe?" Charlotte asked.

"I think so." She tried to remember the exact sequence of events but the process was all still new to her.

"Alright. I'm not far from you. I'll swing by in a few minutes and see if we can figure out what you're doing wrong."

"Thank you so much. I hate to bother you, but I really thought I knew how to use this and it's pretty clear that I don't," Ava sighed, before adding, "Just let yourself in when you get here. I'm upstairs."

"Will do." Charlotte responded before hanging up.

A short time later, Charlotte arrived, waving her beaded bracelet-laden wrist at Ava.

"I'm here."

She entered the living room where Ave was kneeling in front of the coffee table holding the pendulum at eye level. Ava blew hard trying to make it move.

"Well, I know for a fact that's not how it works."

Charlotte laughed.

Disgusted, Ava stood with her hands on her hips. "Honestly, I don't know how else to make it move. I cleared my thoughts. I prayed. I put my question out to the universe. What am I doing wrong?"

"I agree, you did all of that," Kassi interrupted, standing alongside Ava. Before Ava could make an introduction, Kassi extended her hand. "Hi, I'm Kassi Scott. You must be Charlotte. I've heard a lot about you."

Charlotte studied Kassi closely. "Ava's told me about you too, and your friend Georgia. She's right, you are a confident one."

Kassi's eyes narrowed, not sure if she had just been insulted. Charlotte smiled. "And also very protective of Ava. I like that."

Charlotte put her purse down on the floor and sat on the couch facing Ava. "Okay. Let's all sit down and see what you're doing. Show me."

Ava took a deep breath and repositioned the pendulum in front of her heart. "So Kassi asked a question and I was trying to get an answer for her. This is exactly what I said. 'I'm putting it out to the universe. Will Kassi get promoted?'"

Ava held the pendulum as still as she could. It did not move, not even a smidgen. She looked over at Charlotte. "See what I mean? Nothing. I'm not sure how I'm supposed to facilitate any messages, if I can't get a simple answer out of the damn thing."

Charlotte's face looked pinched. "Ava, the pendulum isn't a joke. If you think it's not for you, I can take it back. Your energy has to be genuine and you have to ask the right questions for it to guide you. It's really not that complicated."

Ava frowned. She didn't mean to be disrespectful. "I'm sorry, Charlotte."

"You just need to practice." Charlotte softened a little. "Spend time with the pendulum, get acquainted with each other, and relax. This isn't a test. Maybe just hold off asking for guidance for your friends until you've mastered using it for yourself."

"But what's the difference? If I'm as intuitive as you think I am, why can't I help my friends, too?" Ava shrugged.

Charlotte narrowed her eyes. "This isn't about what you know. It's about what the pendulum knows. Please, understand the distinction. It's easy to get carried away and over- confident."

"Alright. Maybe that's what's happening. Will you just help me figure out what I'm doing wrong then?"

Charlotte motioned for Ava to hand her the pendulum and held it in front of her heart.

"First, you start with a prayer." Charlotte's lips moved in silent devotion. "Next, clear your mind. I focus on things that relax me. Once your mind is free from distractions, you formulate your question. 'Will Kassi get a promotion?' is too broad. Be very specific."

Charlotte closed her eyes and became very still. A few

minutes later they opened to stare at the pendulum. "Will Kassi be promoted before summer's end?" Ava watched Charlotte's hand. It held the pendulum steady. Slowly, the pendulum started to swing to the left. *Yes.*

Charlotte continued. "Will Kassi be promoted in July?" Once again, the pendulum was briefly still before it started again, swinging to the right this time. *No.* She tried again. "Will Kassi be promoted in August?" The pendulum moved left. *Yes.*

Kassi clapped her hands together. "No way! Our promotions are always given out in August. It's our fiscal year end. There's no way you would have known that."

Charlotte nodded. "One more thing, so we can settle this once and for all." She paused, repositioning the pink sphere in front of her heart. "Is Ava the rightful owner of this pendulum?"

For several moments, the pendulum was still. Slowly, it started to swing to the left. *Yes.*

Charlotte let out a deep breath and handed it back to Ava. "There you go. There is nothing wrong with this pendulum. Just remember the steps I've told you and you'll be fine."

She stood and grabbed her purse. "I have to get back to work. You'll figure this out, Ava. Remember, answers come from the pendulum, not you. Kassi, it was nice to meet you. And congratulations on your upcoming promotion."

Ava stood and walked Charlotte to the door. "I really

appreciate you coming over. Please don't think I don't understand what you're saying. I do. I'll figure it out," she promised.

Charlotte studied Ava's determined face. "I know you will."

One Year Later

CHAPTER 11

Ava pulled the door firmly behind her, listening for the lock to click. The sun was teasing the horizon one small yellow and orange tentacle at a time. Daybreak was fast approaching, and she still had so much to do before she would greet her first customer. She hurried down the wooden steps and approached the front door of The Tea Cozy.

Business had been steady and brisk at the shop for some time, and with The Tea Cozy's first anniversary just around the corner, Ava finally could enjoy the results of a job well done. The grand opening had been a huge success; a ribbon cutting ceremony with the mayor and Chamber of Commerce president was featured on the front page of the *Wicks Falls Courant*. With that publicity and more, Ava's caffeine haven now had more regular customers than she had ever dared to hope.

Letting herself inside the shop, she turned on the lights and opened the window blinds, surveying the room as she did. Tables set with blue gingham tablecloths and small glass bowls filled with pink sugar packets dotted the main seating area. The wooden floor was freshly swept and the front counter where Ava served her customers was neat and tidy. A light scent of lemons and bleach permeated the air.

"Thank you, Casey," Ava sighed.

An hour later, the sign in the front door read "OPEN," and a warm glow from the interior lights tickled the waning darkness outside. The bells on the front door jingled and a young woman dressed in blue jeans and a pink short-sleeved blouse breezed into the store.

"Ava?" the woman called. "Are you here?"

Poking her head out of the kitchen, Ava looked quizzically at the woman.

"Mary Jane?"

"Ava!" Mary Jane smiled. "You're not going to believe what happened!"

Ava skirted around the shellacked wooden counter to meet her. "Tell me what happened," she said, giving Mary Jane a quick hug hello.

In The Tea Cozy's first week, Mary Jane had walked through the doors and pronounced it exactly the kind of place Wicks Falls needed. "It's so welcoming," she said at the time, "like an old friend. By the way, Aunt Christine said to tell you she wishes you the best of luck and to let her know if you want the recipe for her praline bars."

Ava was grateful to Christine, the waitress from Moreland who had guided her home to Wicks Falls. She would never be able to repay the favor, but looking out for Christine's niece, Mary Jane was a start, and besides, Ava really liked her.

"Eric told me an article I wrote about raising alpacas is just what *South Carolina Monthly* needs to finish the August issue. You were right! Remember at the last Wicked Wednesday you said I had to write about something I felt really connected to and I would be rewarded? Who knew those cute and fuzzy things would be my first feature article?"

"Did I actually say that?" Ava was smug. Wicked Wednesdays had become a Wicks Falls tradition at The Tea Cozy. Two Wednesdays a month, Ava opened up the shop at night to offer pendulum readings for a small fee. Nadine Costa, another Tea Cozy regular, joined Ava to read tarot cards. Gwinnie Bolens would occasionally stop by too, to read palms, but everyone knew Gwinnie made up most of what she said. It was strictly a BYOB affair, and Ava provided cheese and crackers and any leftover baked goods. Thankfully, she could count on Casey to come and handle the service in exchange for free readings.

"You did. You know how much I love to knit, and

alpaca fleece is definitely the best fiber to work with. I've always gotten my fleece locally at Bunyan Farms and Peter Bunyan let me spend a day at the farm mixing and mingling with the herd. I got some terrific pictures, and if I do say so myself, the article is pretty good. Once again, you were right. Listen, I'm on my way to the magazine for final edits, but I'll see you later. I just wanted to let you to know."

Mary Jane turned to leave but Ava grabbed her arm gently. "Wait a minute. You need some green tea to keep you focused today. Let me pour you a cup to go."

Behind the counter Ava fiddled with the large silver carafes that lined the back wall. She pulled an insulated cup off a stack next to the carafes and dropped a green tea bag into it before pushing it under a spigot. She pulled the lever, allowing steaming water to fall into the cup, handing it to Mary Jane when it was full.

"Here you go, my friend. This should keep you on track today."

Mary Jane smiled, pulling her wallet from a worn brown leather backpack, but Ava stopped her. "This one's on me. Go and finish that article. I can't wait to read it!"

Without a word, Mary Jane smiled at Ava and dashed out the door.

Ava looked around The Tea Cozy and smiled. Instinctively, she touched the sea glass necklace. Her parents would have been so pleased.

"I'm here. I'm here."

Casey Williams came through the door with her arms full of paper towels and cleaning supplies. Ava glanced at the clock above the carafes. It was almost 6:00, but customers would begin arriving any minute.

"Let me help you," Ava said. "You're not that late. Did you get these at DelSanto's?"

"Yeah. I picked them up last night. I figured we'd be out of paper towels before lunch. Sorry, I thought I was on time but Gordie needed to pee right before I was ready to go."

"How is my favorite dog?"

"He's spoiled rotten and he hates when I leave," Casey replied, putting the supplies on the nearest table. "But he's better than any boyfriend I've ever had. He loves me unconditionally, flaws and all."

"Well, don't look at me. I was the one who told you that you and Garrett were perfect for each other. What do I know?" Ava chuckled. For every three or four things she and the pendulum got right, occasionally there would be an epic fail. She thought for sure the energy around Casey and Garrett was perfect, but the universe had said otherwise.

Casey pushed her bangs from her forehead and pulled a scrunchie tight around her blonde hair. She was a natural beauty with pale blue eyes, high cheekbones, and a light sprinkling of freckles across her nose. At twenty-one, Ava thought of her as the little sister she had never had. Ava's first hire was undoubtedly one of the smartest decisions she had made since moving to Wicks Falls. Many people had responded to her help wanted ad in the weeks before The Tea Cozy opened, but only a handful fit the bill and Casey was the cream of the crop.

The Tea Cozy was at its most frenzied the day Casey had arrived. Closing the door behind her, she had paused to survey the room. Loud noises reverberated off the walls as drills and saws sang in harmony. Workers in hard hats and tool belts skirted about like cars on the interstate. Unfazed, Casey scanned the room until she spotted Ava seated at the epicenter of it all.

She waved Casey over, and waited for the young woman to reach her. Casey moved through the construction maze with ease, stopping along the way to help out; she returned a dropped hammer to its owner standing high on a ladder before stooping to straighten a drop cloth that threatened to trip boot-clad feet, unaware. Smiling brightly at the workers as she passed, she elicited more than one cheerful response, but Casey barely noticed as she approached Ava's table.

"Hi, I'm Casey Williams. This place is fantastic!"

Ava stood to shake Casey's hand. "Thank you. I'm Ava. As you can see, it's a bit of a mess at the moment, but I have a very definite vision for the place. First though, I need to get the best people on board. Being new to Wicks Falls, I need someone who knows this town and my future customers."

"Well, I'm your girl. I was born and raised here. My family's been in Wicks Falls for almost one hundred years. We go back three generations and my grandparents still live in the house that my grandfather's dad built. The town only has a few thousand residents, and I know most of them,"

Casey laughed. "And if I don't know them, then my parents or one of my brothers do. It's a tight knit community here. Sometimes it's a bit stifling," she admitted, "but most of the time, we're all one big, happy family."

Ava had seen and heard enough. She hired Casey on the spot, every bone in her body telling her it was the right thing to do. But that night, in the quiet of her apartment, she consulted the pendulum just to be sure. She cleared her mind, said a prayer, and fashioned a very specific question. In her heart, she knew that Casey belonged at The Tea Cozy, but did her intuition agree? "I call upon my higher self to answer these questions," she whispered holding the crystal in front of her. "Was I right to hire Casey today?"

Ava held her breath and waited to see which way the pendulum would move. The response was immediate as it swung to the left. *Yes.* The answer came loud and clear. She sighed in relief.

Now, as she watched Casey prepping for the day ahead of them, she felt such gratitude that Casey was a part of her team.

"You did tell me that," Casey nodded. "Maybe some day things will change."

She still remembered the day that she and Garrett had met. Driving down the highway to the beach, she was singing loudly along with the radio when suddenly the car had started to shudder and the dashboard lights blinked alerting her to check the engine. Pulling over to the side of the road, she grabbed her cell phone to call her brother Cody for help. As she waited, a black pickup truck drove slowly past, pausing briefly before backing up to park in front of her. Casey stretched her neck trying to catch a glimpse of the driver as he stepped out of the truck. Dressed in jeans and a plain white t-shirt, he was rugged, of average height, blonde and tan. "Is everything okay?"

Casey assured him she was fine. "My brother will be here any minute," she told him.

"Do you want me to keep you company until he comes? I can wait in my truck if it would make you feel better."

Normally she would never have accepted his offer, but something about him put her at ease. "Thanks. I guess chivalry isn't dead after all," Casey answered. "You don't have to wait in your truck, but I'll just sit here on the hood of my car so my brother can see me." She stuck out her hand. "I'm Casey by the way."

He took her hand in his, smiling broadly. "Hi Casey. I'm Garrett."

And that's how it began. For more than a year things were good. They had fun together at the beach, going out at night, and hanging out with friends. Casey loved his loyalty to his buddies, but sometimes when he was with them he acted so childish and after a while she had had enough.

"I still love him, but Garrett needs to grow up. I want to be his girlfriend not his babysitter."

"I know. But you're both still young, and guys always seem to mature more slowly than girls. I know you hate to hear that, but it's true. In the meantime, just focus on yourself."

The front door bells jingled again and a tall man with an athletic build and blond hair entered the café. He grabbed a newspaper from the stack next to the door and folded it carefully before tucking it into a messenger bag hanging from his shoulder.

"What's going on here?" he said in a soft voice. "I thought you'd already have my coffee and muffin ready to go." He winked at the women and looked at his watch. "It's almost seven and I'm running late."

Ava grinned at her favorite customer, happy as always to see her friend. "I'll get that for you, Ted," she said, snapping a lid onto a steaming cup of coffee. "You're earlier than usual, so how can you be late? Busy day at the office?"

"Yeah, it's going to be a crazy day." Ted frowned.

He grabbed his order from Ava, handing her money in exchange. "I can't wait. I'm starving, I need a bite now." He reached into the bag for his muffin. "Hey, how come there are two in here? Bonus muffin?"

"I thought you might need it." Ava was matter of fact. "I put a shot of espresso in your coffee, too, for an extra boost."

"You're the best, Ava."

"Anything for you, my friend. Now get going." She shooed him out the door. "I don't want to make you later than you already are."

Waving his thanks, Ted rushed out the door much like

the day they had met. He had come into The Tea Cozy looking for scones. "Do you have any?" he had asked in a panicked voice.

"Of course, we have scones. Blueberry, orange, cinnamon, and raisin. Which one would you like?" Ava asked.

"I want them all," he replied.

"Wow. You must be hungry," she teased. Ava grabbed a white pastry box and a sheet of tissue to place in the bottom and began filling it with scones.

"Well, yes. But they're not for me. I promised the guys at work that I'd bring in scones if UNC beat Duke. I was sure Duke was going to win that game."

"Football?" Ava asked.

"No, chess," Ted replied and laughed when Ava looked at him confused. "Of course, football! The guys at my company take their college football very seriously."

"I see." Ava nodded her head. "Good thing they don't want croissants. I'm just about out of those. And I'm the only game in town. No pun intended."

She handed him the box of scones and smiled. "If you keep losing bets, I might gain myself another regular customer."

"Oh, I'll be back. But next time, I'm just ordering one muffin and a coffee."

"I'll look forward to it." True to his word, Ted had returned a few days later and every day since, grabbing breakfast and chatting with Ava before heading to the office. It was a routine Ava looked forward to and their coffee shop-friendship had blossomed one petal at a time as they shared details of their lives with each other. Ava learned that Ted's family had lived in Wicks Falls for decades. His parents were now retired and his only sibling, Susannah, lived a few houses away from them. They were a close family; he talked about them often as he recounted stories from his childhood.

On a morning when The Tea Cozy was quiet, still too early for the breakfast crowd, Ted casually told Ava he was gay. He studied her face carefully to gauge her reaction. Ava knew he was single, like her, and had never been married, but she had assumed he was just too busy for a relationship.

Telling his family was one of the hardest things he had ever done he told her. He knew Susannah would be fine with it, but his parents were another story entirely. They were of a generation that might not accept his coming out quite as easily. But he should not have worried.

"Ted, Honey," his mother had spoken first as his dad stood silently beside her, "you're our son. We love you. Nothing you say or do could ever change that." Before he could respond, his father had stepped forward and wrapped him in a giant bear hug.

"You're a lucky guy to have such a supportive family," Ava had envied him and the conversation had ended there.

The next few hours flew by as Ava and Casey served dozens of customers. It was a constant stream of tea, coffee, and conversation. Most were regulars, but every so often a stranger wandered in looking for breakfast and a respite from the heat. But no matter who you were, when you stepped into The Tea Cozy, it was like being invited into Ava's home.

Right before lunch, Ava greeted Dayna Harte from Sweet Carolina Real Estate as she approached the counter. A tall woman in her mid-twenties, she wore slim, green dress slacks and a printed silk blouse. The sides of her mouth dipped with concern.

"Hi girls," she said pulling a wallet out of her purse. "Is Charlotte's order ready? It's for those clients I was telling you about who are looking at that huge commercial property in the industrial park. We have a presentation shortly and she wants to make sure we keep everyone's blood sugar elevated. Otherwise, they'll get that 'glazed over' look."

Casey laughed as she grabbed two large brown paper bags and an insulated carafe. "This should do the trick. We have pastries, muffins and a few chocolate treats. And here's some chamomile tea to counteract the sugar high. Isn't it lunchtime? Won't your clients want something more substantial? I can make sandwiches for you."

Dayna shook her head, "No, we don't want a full lunch yet. That will just make them sleepy. If a little sugar and carbs get them in a buying mood then Charlotte will be happy with me." She rolled her eyes. "We all know you don't want to get on Charlotte's bad side."

"Do you want me to deliver them?" Casey asked, coming from behind the counter.

"No thanks," Dayna replied. "I think I can manage. Wish me luck; I have a bonus riding on this sale and I could really use some extra money right now. God, I'm going to hate having to wait for them to decide."

Ava stepped forward, adding napkins and Styrofoam cups to the pile. "Tell Charlotte it will all work out fine. I talked to her on the phone yesterday and she mentioned the meeting, so I consulted my pendulum. But, I'm guessing she already knows the deal will go through." Ava winked as if she were an accomplice in the deal.

"What does that even mean?" Dayna wondered, shrugging her shoulders. "You and Charlotte and all of your 'signs from the universe.' Don't you think it's a little silly to think that a gut feeling and a piece of stone hanging from a chain should dictate how you make decisions? And you know I mean that in the nicest way."

"No offense taken." Ava smiled, studying Dayna. "You know, the universe has a plan for all of us. If you ever change your mind, let me know. We'd love you to come to a Wicked Wednesday. It's a lot of fun, and I could do a consultation for you."

"Yeah, okay. Don't hold your breath." Dayna bundled all of the packages into her arms and headed for the front door. "See you tomorrow," she called over her shoulder.

CHAPTER 12

Ava napped in the comfort of the cushioned window seat, where the afternoon sun was a weightless blanket on her shoulders. Moments like these were rare at The Tea Cozy, so she grabbed them whenever she could. The bell above the front door chimed as someone entered the store. Through slit eyes, she peeked to see who it was.

"Hey, Ted." She welcomed him inside, stretching as she stood, her arms arching long and high above her head.

Ted hesitated in the doorway, confused. "I'm sorry, are you closed?" He looked around at the empty tables. "I can come back later."

"Don't be silly." Ava gestured for him to come in. "I'm

just enjoying the quiet while I can. It doesn't get this way very often." She patted the seat next to her in invitation. "Join me? I was just about to have an iced tea."

"If you're sure I'm not disturbing you?"

With a shake of her head, Ava moved to get their drinks. "I'd love the company."

She disappeared into the kitchen while Ted made himself comfortable in the seat she had just vacated and waited for her to return. A copy of *South Carolina Monthly* rested on the seat beside him. Picking it up, he flipped casually through the magazine's glossy pages.

"I'm surprised to see you here this time of day," Ava called out from the kitchen.

"Another rarity," he answered back. "I never leave work during the day unless I have a meeting or something. There's always something pressing in the world of finance."

"I hear you." Ava sat beside him expertly balancing a tray holding glasses of iced tea and a heaping plate of oatmeal raisin cookies. "These are hot out of the oven," she said strategically placing the warm baked goods on the table in front of him.

"So then why are you here?"

"Oh my God, these are good!" The melting cookie delighted all of his senses. Ted sighed happily and grabbed another, and two more after that, before sharing the plate with Ava. "Sorry, didn't mean to hog them all." He grinned, sheepishly.

"Help yourself," she urged.

"I needed some air," he finally answered between bites. "Clear my head, focus. But if I'd known about these," he said polishing off another cookie, "I'd have been here sooner. How did you know they're my favorite?"

Ava laughed, popping a piece of warm, chewy cookie into her mouth. She knew almost everything about him. Too bad he was gay. He was perfect for her in every way.

"Chalk it up to woman's intuition. Also, I'm pretty sure you mentioned it one or ten times." Her brow arched as she teased him. "Subtlety really isn't your strong suit."

"Hmmm." With his mouth full, she could not tell if Ted was agreeing with her or not. He washed the cookie down with a long slow sip of his drink.

"You know, your brown spot gets larger when you're joking." He smirked with knowing amusement. "It's a dead giveaway."

"You're crazy." But her contemptuous snort said otherwise. She stared at her hands and refused to meet his gaze.

The distinctive brown fleck in Ava's left eye was like a secret hiding in plain sight. Months, even years, went by sometimes before a friend would notice and ask about it.

"Hey, do you know you have two different color eyes?"

"Actually," she'd reply, "I have one eye that's two colors: hazel with a brown spot. I was born this way," Ava would continue already anticipating their follow up questions; they were always the same. "Nothing happened, it wasn't an accident. No, it doesn't hurt. Yes, I see exactly the same with both eyes."

Like Kassi and Georgia, Ted had noticed it right away, the first time they met. "I love your eyes," he'd said, catching her off guard as he paid for his box of scones. His clear blue gaze locked with hers. "They're different. Beautiful," he added.

She'd blushed, surprised and more than a little pleased; he was a good-looking guy, after all. Leaning over the counter, Ava's voice was low as she whispered conspiratorially, "It's my super power. I can read people's minds."

A self-proclaimed Doubting Thomas of such things, of course he did not believe her for a minute, and yet, it was hard not to. Ava's face was an open book, every thought obvious in her expression. It felt wrong not to believe her, but then it had happened, her eye changed color. Ted watched, fascinated as the brown fleck spread over the hazel iris like a can of spilled paint.

Changing the conversation, Ted held up the magazine he had tossed aside earlier, and pointed to its cover story. "Alpacas in South Carolina, now that's news."

"It is." Ava was thoughtful. "Where do you think Mary Jane came up with the idea?"

Ted's snort said he was not buying it. "Wait, you're telling me that you told Mary Jane to write about alpacas?"

"Well, not exactly. But I did tell her that what sets popular feature writers apart from others is a special kind of thinking. More than anything, she wants to be recognized as a great writer, maybe even have her own byline someday. If that's her goal, then Mary Jane needs to make some changes in her life rather than waiting for it to happen to her."

"I'd call that common sense."

Ava looked him square in the eye like a bull ready to charge. Clearly, she disagreed.

Ted smiled. Debates with her were always fun but in this instance, not without risk. Lightening fast, he grabbed another cookie before she pulled the plate away.

Ignoring his slight-of-hand, Ava continued. "I'm just saying, we're all experts when it comes to fixing other people's problems, don't you think?" Opening his mouth to answer, Ava shushed him. "You know I'm right. It's easier to be objective and think clearly for someone else. But when it's our own problem, well that's a different story. Our emotions kick in. We get scared or confused, angry even. And everything gets muddy. So, call it whatever you want. What I gave Mary Jane was clarity...with a little help from a friend."

Ava relaxed in her seat and waited for Ted to catch on.

"Hold on. Are you talking about your pendulum nonsense again? Aw, Ava, how can you believe in that bullshit? You're such a smart woman."

"Excuse me?" She hated him mocking her. "Just because you don't understand, it doesn't mean what the pendulum does isn't real. Would you say that about someone's religion? Do you really think that praying the rosary, for instance, can make things happen? Are you going to tell Catholics that their rosary beads are bullshit? Because what's the difference? In the end, people use whatever tools necessary to support their beliefs. Are you qualified to sit and judge everyone?"

The conversation was going south fast. Ted worked quickly to dial it back. *You really have to think before you speak, Buddy.*

"I'm sorry I upset you," he said, his forlorn expression melting her heart.

Ava pulled her emotions into check. Friends didn't treat each other like this.

"Okay, I'm sorry, too. It's just that the pendulum is part of my life. I don't expect you to accept it but I hope that you're at least respectful of what it means to me. Besides, I hate arguing with you. You were my first friend in Wicks Falls, you know. And now you're one of my best friends."

Ted agreed.

"More than that. Family. You, Kassie, Georgia, and Casey, you four are my family. And, if you were ever stuck, or had a problem, I hope you'd let me help you."

"I'd let you bake me cookies," he teased, doing his best to make her laugh.

With an exasperated smile, she pushed the cookie plate back within his reach. "You're impossible."

"But charming. Besides, you don't have to worry about me," he assured her, holding up his right hand. He pointed to the silver band on his finger. "It was my grandfather's," he said proudly. "I found it the other day tucked in my drawer; I must have put it there for a reason, but I'll be damned if I can remember why." Ted seemed puzzled. "Anyway, I'm wearing it now, for luck."

CHAPTER 13

Ava held Ted's hand, admiring the thick platinum band; heavy brushed metal boldly topped with a smooth square of midnight onyx, it was most definitely a man's ring.

"It's very handsome," she said pointing to the center stone as she moved in for a closer look. "Is that hematite?"

"I'm not sure." He pulled the ring from his finger, handing it to Ava. "Can you tell?"

Ava studied the ring carefully, twisting it between her fingers, holding it up to the light for a better look. The dark stone glimmered sleek and hard. "I'm not positive, but I'm pretty sure it's a blood stone," she said handing it back to him.

"Blood stone? Not sure I like the sound of that." Ted wrinkled his nose, making Ava laugh again.

"Not real blood, silly. See, hematite is shiny black on the outside, like this." She grabbed Ted's hand and pointed to the ring now securely back on his finger. "But inside it's deep red or, 'blood red,' " she said, curling her fingers into air quotes. "Hematite's a pretty powerful crystal, too. I wonder if your grandfather knew that."

Ted shrugged, trying to imagine his conservative-minded grandfather believing in anything besides an honest day's work. "Powerful how?"

"Hematite has a strong physical energy that's great for keeping a person grounded, and it has a slew of other healing properties as well — everything from relieving leg cramps to alleviating fevers."

"If it works on sore muscles, maybe I should start wearing it to the gym." Ted crossed his arms into a muscular torso stretch.

"It couldn't hurt, I suppose," she replied, playing along, "but I think Hematite's healing powers are intended for more serious injuries or illnesses."

He looked at his hand where the ring still gleamed. "It belonged to my Grandpa Clyde," Ted explained. "He gave it to me on my eighteenth birthday."

"*Son,*" Ted's voice dropped low, echoing his grandfather's deep baritone. "*This ring represents everything I believe in. It was a reward to myself for always working hard, staying honest, and never losing sight of what's really important. I want you to have it."*

Ted toyed with the ring, loose enough to spin around his finger without pinching the skin beneath. "I would have been okay with a car," he said wistfully.

Ava laughed. "I'm sure, but I bet you're happy to have it now."

"Absolutely." Ted's teeth flashed white. "Grandpa Clyde was the best, but man could he talk. Sometimes Susannah and I would hide from him just to avoid one of his long-winded lectures. We both adored him anyway. I'm surprised I haven't told you about him before." Ted's gaze grew distant remembering his grandfather. "You know, when he was my age, he sank everything he had into this small-time newspaper in North Carolina. It was a huge gamble for anyone, but especially for a man with a wife and child, and another baby on the way."

"What happened?" Ava loved a good story. She folded her arms comfortably on the table in front of her and waited for him to continue.

"Well, he worked day and night, 365 days a year for too many years, according to my grandmother. Eventually, though, he turned that small, failing newspaper into the region's leading daily publication. By 1929, my grandfather was not only a man of means, but a well- respected one as well." Ted paused here for effect. "He was also very lucky."

"Go on."

He smiled at his captivated audience and explained. "A couple of months before the Big Crash, my grandfather sold all of his stock holdings. He made a killing that practically doubled his fortune. Unlike so many others whose lives were destroyed right after that." Ted's voice cracked with emotion. "But not Grandpa Clyde's, thank God."

Ava gave him a second before asking, "What made your grandfather sell when he did?"

Ted groaned. "I was afraid you'd ask that," he said, avoiding her quizzical expression.

"Why?"

"My grandfather always said there was no rhyme or reason to what he did. He just had a feeling."

"I like this man!" She grinned. "Tell me more."

"That's it, really. He went with his gut and sold all of his stock for a gazillion dollars and then used it to expand the business into the empire it is today."

Finished with his story, Ted rested comfortably against the cushions and sipped his drink.

"So, Miller Publishing, that's you?" Surprised, Ava scrutinized her friend, wondering what other secrets the handsome thirty-something man was hiding. "How did I not know this?"

"Not me, my family," Ted was quick to correct her. "I went a different route. I don't want any special favors or helping hands; I want to succeed, or fail, on my own so I keep the family name pretty quiet. It seems to be working for me, too. You know my boss, Charlie?"

"Large hot coffee, black, with a warm cinnamon roll." Ava barely had to think about it. She knew the names of all of her regular customers, but more importantly, she knew their preferred orders.

"Well, Charlie treats me like the son he never had. When he retires, he wants me to take over. This is all down the road mind you, but he's grooming me now to be ready when the time comes." Ted was confident. "Time and training, that's all I need."

"And don't forget the ring!" Ava beamed.

"What do you mean?"

"Well, besides physical healing, hematite has other nutritive powers as well."

He stared at her, blankly.

She explained further. "Hematite is also very calming, and it can boost self-confidence." She cocked her head to one side to look at him. "Not that you need it."

Holding his hand out in front of him, Ted stared at his grandfather's ring. "So, it sounds like Grandpa Clyde's ring has some pretty special powers. . . .just like your pendulum."

"So you agree, they both have powers?" She countered, without missing a beat. "Because that's all that really matters, believing in the ring."

Ted bit into a cookie, chewing slowly, and buying time as

he chose his next words with care. He and Ava would never see eye-to-eye on this, but it was hardly worth losing their friendship over. He had been kidding about the ring, but to her, it was no joking matter. If you doubted the pendulum, you doubted her, too.

"A toast," he said at last, raising his glass between them. "To the power of believing…in something or someone." He touched his glass to Ava's, noting the upward curve of her lips, the happy glint in her eyes, and relaxed. A happy medium had been reached, for now at least.

CHAPTER 14

Raspberry and vanilla mingled with the scents of baking bread and brewing coffee as Ava entered The Tea Cozy's kitchen where Casey moved purposefully, transferring muffins and pastries from the twin convection ovens to a tower of cooling racks.

"Good morning!"

Placing a pale lavender apron over her head, Ava pulled the strings tight around her waist. A quick check of the room told her that Casey had been there for a while already.

"You've been busy," she said. "How can I help?"

Moving to the center of the room, Casey kneaded a pale mound of dough on the block granite island, flipping the soft disk over and in several times before letting it rest.

"I think we're in pretty good shape, right now."

With a floured finger, she pointed to the stacked cooling racks loaded with freshly baked pastries. Casey inventoried her morning accomplishments one by one. "Muffins, check. Scones, check. Croissants, check. One batch of cinnamon rolls is in the oven and I'm finishing up this last batch." Grabbing a nearby rolling pin, she began flattening the dough in front of her.

"That's plenty," Ava agreed, once again giving silent thanks for Casey. It had to have been more than luck that brought the young woman into her life. In Casey, Ava had a loyal and hardworking employee, and even better, she had a true friend. Filling a mug with steaming, rich coffee, she joined Casey at the workstation. "Looks like you've got the morning crowd covered. I'll take care of lunch and afternoon snacks. What do you think? Something cool and simple? Ray Band, the weather guy, says it's going to be another scorcher out there today." She giggled. The name of the local meteorologist got her every time.

"A perfect beach day!" Casey agreed, trying hard but failing to keep the excitement out of her voice. Feeling Ava's questioning gaze upon her, she shrugged, a shy smile spreading across her face.

"Garrett asked me to go to the beach with him today." Casey hid her blushing cheeks in her work, as she smoothed the pastry roller over an expanse of dough-covered table.

"Garrett? When did he call you?"

Ava knew Casey thought of her ex-boyfriend as "the one that got away." Just like every other couple on Earth, she and Garrett had had their problems, but they had also really loved each other. As her boss turned friend and confidante, Ava had listened to Casey pour her heart out sharing the good, the bad, and finally the ugly details of her relationship. She had not wanted to break up with Garrett, but he had left her no choice with his immature ways.

"I ran into him at the gas station the other day. He was at the next pump, and we just started talking. It was nice."

Casey was nonchalant as she popped the tray of cinnamon rolls into the waiting oven to bake. Setting the timer for thirty-five minutes, she focused on cleaning up the kitchen. As Ava watched, Casey gathered up the dirty dishes, washing them in hot, soapy water before drying and putting them all away. Casey's small biceps flexed as she moved on to power cleaning the granite baking counters, scraping bits of batter and sticky dough from their surfaces, and scrubbing the appliances into stainless steel mirrors. Satisfied she had restored sparkle and order to the kitchen, she poured herself a cup of coffee and joined Ava at the island.

"It was easy and fun, the way it used to be," she said, picking up the conversation where she had left off. "When we first started dating."

Ava smiled and sipped her coffee, letting Casey have the floor.

"He left first, and I thought that was it until he called

that night and asked me to have dinner with him."

"Where did he take you?"

"Harvest."

Ava released a low, slow whistle. "Nothing says romance like Harvest. Sounds to me like someone's trying to win you back."

"I hope so." Casey tugged on her ponytail, the blonde strands wrapping around her finger like a spool of thread. "What do you think, should I give him another chance?"

Ava was quiet, as she stirred her coffee and contemplated the question. "I think you need to be careful," she said, deciding not to sugar coat it. "Garrett's already disappointed you before. Getting back together could just cause more heartache. On the other hand, he seems to have really missed you, too. Maybe not being together for a while helped him grow up and appreciate what you two had together."

Casey nodded. Ava had a knack for seeing things clearly. "I know that's what I want, to be with Garrett again. I just wish I had some kind of guarantee that he's really ready to be with me, too."

A comfortable silence settled over them both as Ava and Casey retreated into their private thoughts. After a moment, Ava offered, "I could ask the pendulum again, if you want. Maybe it was right the first time and you are meant to be together."

"Really? You'd do that?"

"Of course, I will," Ava replied. "I wouldn't have offered otherwise. Besides, I want to know as much as you do if Garrett is the guy for you."

"You're the best!" Casey wrapped Ava in a python-like squeeze. "Thank you, Ava. I owe you big time."

"No problem," Ava wheezed. "Just call me a sucker for love." Recognizing the familiar chime of the front door bell, she gently extricated herself from Casey's tight embrace, smoothing the creases from her now wrinkled apron with her hands. "Now that we've got that figured out, what do you say we get back to work?"

CHAPTER 15

The next day, Casey hurried into The Tea Cozy just as Ava flipped the sign on the door to read "Open," leaving her no time to ask if Ava had managed to consult the pendulum. But after the perfect afternoon she and Garret had spent together at the beach, she was willing to bet what it would say. Everything about their date had felt right, and she was hopeful that just maybe they could work things out.

"You're early, Honey." Ava called, spotting Casey from the kitchen. "I don't have you on the schedule until twelve o'clock."

"Ellie texted me last night and asked if I would cover for

her," Casey replied, swapping out her jean jacket for an apron with 'The Tea Cozy" embroidered on it. "She's picking her son up at the airport today."

Ava smiled warmly. "You're a peach. I'm sure Ellie was very appreciative. Her son doesn't get back home very often, and I know she can't wait to see him."

"It's no problem. I don't mind covering for her." Grabbing a tray of muffins to take up front, Casey gave Ava a friendly nudge as she passed by. "Besides, you know I love being here. Are we ready to rock and roll?"

Wiping her hands clean on a towel, Ava headed towards the front door. "Almost."

From the center of the room, Ava took in the warm tones of the smoky quartz walls and the prisms of refracted light cast by the multitude of crystals hanging in the front windows. The whole café had evolved over the year to convey serenity, a space to nurture the soul. With closed eyes, she readied herself for the daily blessing, a ritual she had started the day The Tea Cozy opened. 'If you don't ask, you don't get,' her father had taught her long ago. So every day she prayed, "Bless this day and help me to help others."

She opened her eyes slowly, wiggling her shoulders where the skin between them prickled uncomfortably. Something didn't feel right. *That's strange*, she thought. Ava looked around. Nothing was out of place. Everything appeared to be in order.

"Okay," she said to Casey, brushing off the unsettled feeling. "I guess we're ready."

The busy morning ended uneventfully when the post office clock chimed twelve; lunch hour had officially begun.

"Hi, girls. What's new?" Charlotte asked as she breezed through the door with a wave that made her trademark beaded bracelets clink together. "Ah. Thank God for air conditioning." She plucked delicately at the cotton blouse clinging to her chest. "I feel like I just stepped out of a sauna."

"Charlotte! I was wondering when we'd see you again. It seems like Dayna's now the official courier for Sweet Carolina Realty."

"Sorry, Ava." Charlotte apologized for her absence. "Things have been crazy at the office lately. We've had a rush of snowbirds looking for winter places. It never fails. They come in bursts, everyone looking for that undiscovered, bargain piece of property at the same time."

"Well, I can't blame anyone for falling in love with Wicks Falls' southern charm," Ava empathized. "By the way, how'd you make out on that big deal a few weeks ago? The one we talked about. Dayna told us about it, too."

"The Wharton deal?"

"I'm not sure. It was the big commercial property in the industrial park. She came by to pick up a big order and said she would get a bonus if things went well. I told her to tell you that things looked good. It was just a feeling, but to be certain, I consulted the pendulum."

Charlotte smiled approvingly. "Yes, that was the

Wharton deal. And yes, Dayna gave me your message." She laughed at Ava's eager expression. "And yes again, you were right. We closed the deal above asking price. Sounds like someone's getting the hang of the pendulum."

"Hey, I might have had a rocky start last year, but I think I've got a pretty good handle on things now. Like you said, it's a process. I just have to keep my mind clear and be completely open to whatever comes through. But I gotta tell you, it doesn't always make sense to me."

"And maybe it won't," Charlotte agreed, "because you don't always know everything there is to know. That's the point, that's why it's so important to pass on the messages exactly as you read them, just like I told you. It's up to the person you're reading for to put all of the information together for themselves."

Ava bowed to Charlotte. "I promise you I'm not just sharing my own advice, unless of course someone asks for it," she added. "Then I give them my opinion."

"Good." Charlotte nodded firmly. She worried about Ava's Wicked Wednesdays. Charging for a pendulum reading? Why not just go to a fortune-telling booth at a carnival?

"Well, today I don't need your advice. I'm actually here for a little pick-me-up. May I have a sweet tea and a chocolate croissant to go, please?"

"You got it." She turned to Casey at the register. "Honey, can you grab a chocolate croissant and a sweet tea for Charlotte?"

"Sure thing, boss. One chocolate flake and a tall cold one on the fly, coming right up."

"Thank you." Ava chuckled and turned back to Charlotte. "God bless that girl. I sleep well at night knowing she's here helping me."

"I've known Casey since she was little," said Charlotte, walking with Ava to the register. "You don't have to sell me on her virtues."

"So what else is. . . ." Before Ava could finish, the door opened, and Ted walked in.

"Well, look who it is," she said, a wide smile spreading across her face. "Mr. Don't Return My Calls Or Texts. I was starting to get a complex you know. You even blew me off for Tuesday Night Thai last night."

Charlotte turned her head as Ted shuffled in to The Tea Cozy, his phone extended in front of him so he could read it.

"What?" He asked, barely acknowledging either woman.

"Where've you been?" Ava tried again. "I had your coffee ready per usual this morning. You never showed."

"Sorry." He shrugged, unapologetically. "I had to get to the office early this morning. No time for breakfast."

"You must be working on some pretty important stuff to miss my coffee," Ava chided. She turned to Charlotte. "You know Ted Miller, don't you? He works for Charlie Harper."

Charlotte smiled, extending her hand. "We've met. It's good to see you again, Ted. How's my friend Charlie? How are things at Harper?"

"Good. Busy, but good." He looked at Ava, letting go of Charlotte's hand. "Can I get that coffee now?"

"Sure. How about a sandwich, too? You seem a little distracted. Food will help you focus." She waited for him to answer, but Ted was once again engrossed in his phone.

"Great. A turkey sandwich it is. I'll be right back." Nodding to Charlotte, Ava shot her a "talk to him" look and hurried off to the kitchen. Charlotte cleared her throat.

"So, Ted, what are you working on these days? Anything exciting?"

"Um…well…you know, a little of everything," he answered vaguely.

Undeterred, Charlotte continued. "Charlie certainly has built Harper Technologies into a cutting-edge company. I remember when he started the company it was just a small office with one employee, and Charlie. Now it's one of Wicks Falls' corporate stars. You must love working there."

"Uh huh," he answered, his head down.

Moments later, Ava reappeared carrying two paper bags and two beverages. Placing them on the counter she said, "Okay, Charlotte, your sweet tea and croissant come to four dollars and thirty-two cents."

Charlotte handed her five dollars, waving away the change.

"Ted, your sandwich and coffee are seven dollars even. I

added some American cheese and lettuce and tomato to cover all four major food groups," she joked.

Ted clicked his phone off, slipping it into his pocket. "Oh, okay."

Their hands touched as he gave Ava ten dollars. She flinched as she took the money from him.

"Here you go, handsome," she said, placing his change on the counter. "Will I see you for breakfast tomorrow, or are you a lunch regular now?"

"No, no." Grabbing his order and his change, Ted turned to leave. "I'll be back in the morning." He left without saying good-bye.

"You saw that, right?" Charlotte barely waited for him to leave before asking.

"What?" Ava asked.

"You know exactly what I'm talking about, Ava. I saw your face when he handed you the money. And I felt it when I shook his hand. Be careful, Ava. That kind of negative energy can be transferred."

Before Ava could reply, Charlotte picked up her bag and drink. "Don't say I didn't warn you."

CHAPTER 16

Ted left The Tea Cozy for Harper Technologies, balancing his sandwich and coffee in one hand, his phone in the other. It beeped, drawing his attention to the text message showing on the screen.

"Damn it," he swore softly, accelerating his pace.

Ten minutes later, he slipped unnoticed into his office, closing the door quietly behind him. From his leather chair, Ted checked the phone screen again. He typed a short reply, "No. But I will."

He pulled the freshly made sandwich from its bag barely noticing the smiley face Ava had drawn on the wrapper hoping to boost his spirits. Going to The Tea Cozy had been a mistake. He did not have time for Ava's concern or Charlotte's nosiness. That woman made him feel uncomfortable, like she knew something he did not. Why Ava was friends with her was beyond him.

The phoned beeped again, knotting his stomach into a hard ball as Ted finished his lunch. "I told you, I will," he typed. The phone beeped back almost immediately. "Tonight," he promised. "I have it, don't worry."

Shit. He flipped the phone face down on his desk, staring blankly at the computer monitor in front of him. The brightly lit desktop glowed blue. Ted pulled a key from his pocket to unlock the desk drawer beside him. Reluctantly, he thumbed through its contents one cream colored folder after another, hesitating, as if he did not already know that what he searched for was hiding in the drawer's deepest recesses, and as if he did not know that he was the one who put it there in the first place. Carefully, he pulled the file from the drawer and discreetly placed it on the desk where only he could see it.

He worked quickly. A few strokes of the keyboard, some creative figuring and the deed was done. Shame and fear gnawed at his gut in unison. "This is the last time," he promised himself as he returned the folder to the locked drawer. "It has to be."

A loud knock sounded on his office door. Already jumpy, it startled him from his chair. *Jesus!* He gripped the edge of the desk for support. "Come in."

Charlie Harper, founder and president of Harper Technologies, wore his sixty plus years well. Tall and lean in

114

khaki slacks and a pink collared shirt, only his balding head with its neatly trimmed fringe of gray and a slight softening in his mid-section gave proof to his actual age. That and the reading glasses semi-permanently perched on the end of his patrician nose.

"Hey, Ted. Have a minute?" He checked to see if Ted was alone.

"Sure, Charlie. Come on in." Ted struggled to keep his tone casual. It was not unusual for Charlie to drop in unexpectedly. There was always some aspect of the business to discuss. But his timing was unnerving. "What's on your mind?"

Charlie closed the door behind him, taking a seat in front of Ted's desk. "I wanted to talk to you about Synthesis. How are we looking on the budget for implementing that software? I talked to Mike Belcourt about it yesterday, and he's eager to understand what the anticipated costs are now that we're getting close to the conversion date."

As Charlie spoke, Ted forced himself to relax and breathe. "Um. Yes. I have that budget just about finalized. I'll pull it up on my computer." He typed with trembling hands, thankful that Charlie couldn't see them, and brought the Synthesis file to his screen. "Let me print it out real quick so we can take a look."

He handed Charlie a copy of the file. "Okay. You can see that we have almost all of the numbers from the field guys. Brian has provided forecasts for expected expenses for both the implementation and the next three years. These numbers are based on a 100% usage capacity, which we know is optimistic but not improbable. A best-case scenario, if you will."

Charlie's head cocked to one side as he flipped through the pages listening to Ted's review of the numbers. "What's the total for conversion expenses? And how many people are we anticipating having on the team?"

"Conversion expenses are right there on page two about midway down." Ted pointed to the information. "The team will have six people including Brian. He's guessing that they'll need a week to get everything up and running and to deal with any glitches." Focusing on the facts, Ted's confidence returned. "Of the six team members, Abbey will oversee two of them exclusively for training. Overall, this is a pretty standard conversion. Brian doesn't anticipate any major problems."

"Good. You know, Mike and I go way back. He's a self-starter like me and built Synthesis from the ground up. I need your assurance that everything will go smoothly, that we've accounted for everything and missed nothing. No surprises. I want Mike to be completely satisfied."

"You have my word," Ted promised. "I'll meet with Brian one more time to make sure every t is crossed and i dotted. I won't let you down."

Ted's phone beeped on the desk where he had left it, the noise seeming to echo off the office walls. Ignoring it, he concentrated on saving and closing the Synthesis budget file until the persistent beeping finally stopped.

"I know you won't, that's why I trust you to get it

right." Charlie was firm. "Let's have this done by end of day tomorrow, okay?"

"You got it. Tomorrow, I'll have it on your desk." Ted glared at the phone, willing it to stay quiet long enough for Charlie to leave.

"I'm not finished." Charlie scowled, surprising Ted.

"Sorry," he muttered his confidence starting to waver under his boss's suddenly stern demeanor.

"You should be." He paused, piercing Ted with a sharp look. "You got us both in some serious trouble."

Fuck! Ted almost threw up. "Charlie, I'm so sorry. I never. . . ."

Rubbing the back of his neck, Charlie silenced Ted with an extended hand. "No, no, Emma was right."

"Mrs. Harper?" *WTF. How did she know?*

"Yeah. She thinks I'm a monster that overworks and underappreciates you." Charlie sighed heavily. "She's not entirely wrong," he admitted. "I do expect a lot of you." Gesturing to their surroundings, he said, "I have to, if I'm going to entrust all of this to you one day."

Charlie's voice cracked, and he pressed a finger to the corner of his eye.

"Dust," he explained, clearing his throat. "So yes, you work long hours. Yes, you're here most weekends, and yes, you prove me right every day for believing in you, and trusting you."

He moved to stand beside a speechless Ted, gripping the younger man's shoulder in his strong hand. Ted flinched, and Charlie frowned. "I know I don't tell you enough, but thank you, Ted. I'm not sure I could keep it all going without you."

Ted was silent, trying to corral his jumbled thoughts bouncing off one another like bumper cars. He had not seen it coming. Every time he had imagined sitting down with Charlie, he had been the one talking, confessing. He liked this version better.

"I'm pretty sure I'm the one who should be thanking you," Ted said, pointing out the irony. "But I have to admit, I love hearing you say it."

Standing to shake Charlie's hand, Ted thanked him, grateful beyond words. "You've given me so much. I want you to know I'll work every day, and night too, to repay you."

"You already have, son." Charlie started to leave. "Oh," he said, turning back to Ted, "I almost forgot. Emma wanted me to invite you to dinner next Thursday. She's worried you don't have a social life because of me. She said to bring a date, female or male." Charlie blushed.

Ted chuckled. "My romantic life's pretty non-existent right now. How about if I bring my friend Ava, from The Tea Cozy?"

"That would be fine. Tell her it's casual. We'll see you at 7:00."

The phone started to beep again. Ted ignored it. "Great. Thanks. We'll be there."

Charlie gave him two thumbs up and pointed to the phone. "You gonna get that?"

"It's okay," Ted replied. "I know who it is. I'll call him back later."

"Your call." With a wave and a smile, Charlie was gone, leaving Ted alone with his phone, beeping yet again.

CHAPTER 17

The post office clock chimed five times, cheerfully signaling the end of the workday for those who still adhered to the traditional 9-to-5. Inside The Tea Cozy, Ava was busy closing out the register, counting and recording first the coins into small pouches marked pennies, nickels, dimes, and quarters; then the bills bound into packets of $1s, $5s, $10s and $20s. Together, they made the blue leather deposit bag bulge. Pleased with the day's earnings, she left the shop, tucking the bag under her arm and locking the door behind her.

It was a short walk from The Tea Cozy to the bank, where she slipped the moneybag into the night deposit slot.

Grasping the drawer's thick steel handle, she pushed it closed, listening for a heavy thump as the deposit bag landed securely inside. Just to be sure, Ava pulled back on the handle again, carefully inspecting the chute's smooth metal lining. Satisfied it was empty, she began a leisurely stroll back to her apartment.

It was a beautiful afternoon in Wicks Falls where rush hour saw more cars in the streets than any other time of day, as business people made their way home to dinner, a sweet tea on the front porch, or maybe even a quick nine holes of golf. On Palm Street, retail shops were still brisk with tourists searching for that perfect souvenir, and sidewalk cafes overflowed with diners enjoying a happy hour cocktail or a meal al fresco. Life was good, she thought, smiling with contentment.

"Oomph!" Ava gasped as something hit her square and hard, putting her balance in jeopardy as the sidewalk rose up to meet her. She put out her hands to break the fall.

"Oh my God, I'm so sorry." Strong hands grabbed her from behind. They pulled her up and planted her firmly on the ground. Having prepared herself for the worst, Ava was just happy to be upright.

"Sorry for saving me? That's just silly." She lifted her gaze to Ted, but he did not share her humor. Pale and concerned, he was too busy scanning Ava for injuries.

"I didn't even see you," he said, mentally kicking himself for flying out of the office like a panicked maniac. His hands were like anchors weighting Ava's arms to her sides in a steady grip that refused to let go. "I wasn't paying attention."

"I'm fine," Ava chuckled, wondering who was supporting whom. She loosened his bruising hold to prove her point. "See?" She twirled slowly, her limbs and yellow A-line skirt following suit. "One hundred percent A-Okay."

Ted took a step back while Ava took stock of his ruffled appearance. The man she sometimes referred to as Mr. GQ was anything but right now. His blond hair flopped across his forehead, its usual smooth neatness jerked out of place by Ted tugging at his tie like it was noose. In a word, he was agitated.

"Hey, you don't look so good." Worried, she guided him to a nearby bench. "Why don't we sit down for a minute?"

"I'm sorry. . . ." Ted started to apologize again, but Ava stopped him.

"You bumped into me, Ted, that's all. No crime committed here." She nudged his shoulder with hers, teasing him. "Where were you going in such a hurry anyway? Hot date?"

She waited for him to answer, expecting a typical Ted response, teasing or suggestive. Instead, he just frowned at her. Ted leaned forward, his forearms pressed into his thighs, his head in his hands.

"Honey, are you okay?" Ava rubbed his back in slow, comforting circles, massaging the knotted muscles beneath his sweat-dampened shirt.

"Ted, what is it? What's wrong?"

"Nothing," he answered at last, his muffled reply barely

reaching her ears. "Or maybe, everything." He turned his head to look at her. "I messed up, Ava. I mean, I really messed up, and now I don't know what to do about it."

Ava continued her quiet soothing, trying to process what he had just told her. She had never seen Ted like this before. It explained a lot for sure, from his moody behavior to his erratic schedule of late. In the past, she could have told time by his clockwork routines. His voicemail was filled with messages she had left him, all unreturned, and texts, too many to count, went unanswered. They had not gone out in forever. In fact, the only place she seemed to see him these days was at The Tea Cozy and then he was always in too much of a hurry to talk.

"Is it work?"

"Sort of. I can't seem to get out of my own way, and it's making everything worse." Reluctant to say more, he changed the subject. "You sure you're alright?"

"You mean from before?" She nodded her head vigorously. "Perfectly fine, thanks to your catch."

"Good." His smile was weak. "At least I did something right today. And I'm glad I ran into you. I've been meaning to ask you something."

"What's that?" She was relieved to see the color returning to his face along with his composure.

Ted straightened and squared his shoulders. "Charlie and Emma Harper have invited us to dinner at their house on Thursday," he said.

"Us? I barely know them." Ava did not try to hide her surprise.

"Well, technically they invited me, but they told me to bring a friend and I'd like that friend to be you. It'll be fun," he promised.

"I'd love to." Ava agreed without hesitation. "And maybe you can even talk to Charlie about what's going on. Off the clock I mean."

A shadow touched Ted's face briefly like a cloud passing over the sun. It was gone before Ava noticed. "Maybe." He squeezed her hand. "I'll pick you up at 6:30."

CHAPTER 18

On a steamy Thursday evening, Charlie Harper greeted Ted and Ava as his wife, Emma, joined them in the foyer.

"Welcome to our home." Emma gave Ted a quick hug before turning to Ava. "And this must be Ava." Her smile was warm and friendly. "I've heard so much about you," she said. "Or should I say, about your cinnamon rolls." She patted her husband's stomach affectionately.

Ava laughed, raising her hands in surrender. "Guilty as charged." She took the gift box Ted had carried in with them and presented it to Emma. "I hope you don't mind. I brought some for you and Charlie. Thank you so much for having us over."

"It's our pleasure." Shorter than Charlie by a head of stylishly short dark hair, Emma stood beside him with one arm hooked around his waist. "My darling husband just needs reminding now and then that everyone needs a break from work and to have some fun," she chastised.

Charlie made a face. "And on that note, who'd like a drink?" Three hands shot into the air, and he nodded approvingly. "Follow me."

Ted and Ava followed Charlie through the plantation-style home to a covered patio in the back. The floor was a colorful mosaic of intricate stonework. From above, a large tobacco-leaf fan waved the evening air around them in scented swirls of wax myrtle, honey suckle, and cardinal flowers.

"This is lovely." Accepting a tall cool drink, the colors of sunset, Ava drank in her surroundings. "And so is this," she said, sipping the sweet and tangy cocktail.

"It's Charlie's signature drink," Ted told her. "Only he knows what's in it, and he's not telling. Careful," he warned as she drank more. "They're delicious, but deadly. Pace yourself."

Charlie snorted. "Don't listen to him Ava. Have you noticed he's become a bit of a worry wart lately?"

"I'm not worried. I'm just looking out for my friend." Ted felt the burn of the potent cocktail sliding down his throat. "Too many of these and we'll be sleeping on your couch tonight."

"I'll look out for Ava." Emma set a plate of hors d'oeuvres on the center table, her loose white tunic top and slacks floating around her as she moved to sit next to her guest. "We girls have to stick together. Right?"

"Right," Ava agreed, touching her glass to Emma's.

"Oh boy, Ted. Do you see where this is going?" Charlie's head shook with mock dismay.

"Yep. Battle of the sexes, and we just got here."

"Oh please," Emma and Ava denied in unison. "We're just having dinner. Where's the battle in that?"

A dubious Charlie took Ted by the elbow. "C'mon, Ted," he said leading the way to a pair of bar stools in the corner. "I think these have our names on them."

Ava watched them go, looking every bit like a father and son in cahoots. What a perfect opportunity for Ted to talk to Charlie about his mysterious problem. She hoped he would.

"Give me a hand with dinner, Ava?" Emma interrupted Ava's thoughts as she made her way into the house. "And don't worry about them," she said, tilting her chin at the men, "They'll be all right without us for a bit."

In the kitchen, Emma made swift work of organizing platters and bowls, mixing dressing, and tossing salad. Ava arranged oven-warmed rolls and biscuits in a sweetgrass basket, placing it on the dinner table with a small dish of chilled butter.

"If you light the candles, I'll call the boys to dinner." Emma handed Ava a book of matches as she left the room. A minute later she was back, with Ted and Charlie at her heels.

"I'm starving!" Ted sniffed at the air trying to discern the delicious aromas. "Emma is the best cook," he told Ava, taking a seat directly across from her. "So what culinary magic have you performed tonight?"

Ava recognized the Prince Charming smile he bestowed upon their hostess. There was not a man, woman, or child alive who did not melt from its warmth, and Emma was no exception.

"You're making me blush," she said, passing a platter of pan-seared salmon drizzled with lemon aioli. "We have rice pilaf and roasted asparagus, too. Don't be shy." She urged them to fill their plates. "There's plenty for seconds."

Charlie poured wine while Emma served until everyone had a full plate and glass in front of them. Taking her seat at the end of the table, she beamed across its length at her husband. "I'm so glad you both could make it tonight," she said to Ava, seated on her right. On her left, Ted felt her soft gaze move to him. "We love having you here."

"We love being here," he answered.

Ava raised her glass. "Thank you so much for having us, and for this delicious meal."

"So, Ava," Emma chatted as they ate, "tell us about The Tea Cozy. What's the inspiration behind it?"

"It's sort of a long story." Ava did her best to avoid

boring them with the details. "But I'd have to say my mother had a lot to do with it. After she passed, my world was turned upside down."

"You know, she used to say the only constant in life is change, and no matter what you do or say, you can't stop it. But I believe that if you embrace change, maybe you can control it a little bit, make it work for rather than against you."

"Change is hard," Emma agreed, "and scary, too, sometimes. But what are you going to do about it?"

"Well. . . ." Ava glanced at Ted. The slow shake of his head was imperceptible to everyone but her. She ignored it.

"It's different for everyone," she continued, speaking to Emma. "Some people are good at managing change. They have a strong sense of self, know exactly what they want in life, and focus on getting it. They're not fazed by anything that's thrown at them. But others aren't always as sure. They don't like change. If the reason it happens isn't clear right away, then sometimes they need help understanding it."

Placing his fork and knife on his empty plate, Charlie dabbed sauce from his lips with a crisp linen napkin. "I'd put Ted and me in the first group," he said.

"But what do you say about the ones who don't like change?" Emma wanted to know.

Ava drank her wine as Ted shifted in his seat waiting for her to answer. "When I first moved to Wicks Falls, I met a woman named Charlotte Boyer." Ted's head dropped in defeat.

"We know Charlotte!" Charlie and Emma exclaimed together.

"Sharp as a tack." Charlie sipped his wine. "And a little intimidating."

"Because she's smart?"

"Because she's Charlotte."

"I agree." Ted supported Charlie.

"Whatever." Emma refused to be distracted. "Go on, Ava." She poured more wine in both of their glasses.

"There is something unique about Charlotte," Ava agreed. "I don't know how to describe it, but she's kind and generous, too. After I bought my home and The Tea Cozy, she gave me something I'd never seen before."

Ava felt like she was at summer camp telling ghost stories, with Emma and Charlie hanging on her every word. Ted sat with his arms crossed, an amused smirk on his face as he listened to her describe the pendulum and what it meant to her.

"I can't say I don't know how I ever got by without it, but now that I have it, I feel more confident in my decisions and actions. It's like somebody saying 'yes, that's the right answer,' on a test. And the best part is that the pendulum helps me to help other people feel the same way."

"That's incredible, Ava." Emma looked at her husband. "Don't you think so, Charlie?"

After Ava's story, Charlie was once again relaxed in his chair. "I'm not really sure what I think about it," he confessed. "I mean, I'm not sure if I believe in the pendulum's truth, as you call it, but I do believe that anything that can make people feel good about themselves or their actions can't be a bad thing."

"That's fair." Emma acknowledged. "What about you, Ted?"

Silent until now, Ted rejoined the conversation, briefly. "I plead the fifth," he said, making everyone chuckle.

"Ted and I have had this conversation a million times," Ava explained. "He's not a fan."

"Well, I am." Emma prided herself on being open-minded. The practice of the pendulum was intriguing to her. "Ava, would you do a reading for me?"

"Anytime," Ava was quick to answer. "You know, we have a thing at The Tea Cozy called Wicked Wednesdays. It's the first and third Wednesday of every month. I do pendulum readings and Nadine Costa reads tarot cards. It's a lot of fun. But if you're looking for something more private, just call me."

After dessert, Ted and Ava took their leave, amid hugs, and thank yous, and 'we'll do this again soon.' Emma gave Ava a final hug and promised to see her soon at The Tea Cozy.

On the car ride home, she gushed to Ted. "I LOVE THEM!"

Ted laughed. "Yeah, they're pretty great."

"I mean Charlie's always very nice when he comes in for his morning coffee, but tonight he was just so much fun. And, Emma -- I really love her. I can't wait to read the pendulum for her."

"Uh huh."

Sensing Ted's lack of interest in that area, Ava changed the subject. "Did you get a chance to talk to Charlie tonight? About what's bothering you, I mean."

"No." The passing streetlights flickered inside the car illuminating, Ted's chiseled profile.

"Why not? Charlie was in a great mood, and he clearly adores you. I thought it was the perfect opportunity to tell him everything."

Ava sensed a shift in Ted like a drop in temperature. She waited for him to speak, but it was no use, he was shutting her out. His silence was an impenetrable barrier between them, and it hurt.

"Maybe I could help," she offered quietly, biting her lip. "You know, ask the pendulum."

"Forget it." Ted kept his eyes on the road.

Ava shot him a withering glance. *What a jackass.* Sometimes she wondered why she even bothered.

Her expression told Ted he'd crossed the line. "I'm sorry, Ava." He softened. "It seems like that's all I've been saying lately. I'm sorry. But, I really mean it."

They pulled up to Ava's apartment and Ted put the car in park. Ava could not contain herself any longer. "What the hell is going on, Ted?" She blurted. "I'm your best friend for Christ's sake. Why won't you tell me?"

"I can't." Ted leaned over to open her door and kissed her softly on the cheek. "Thank you for coming with me tonight," he said. "And thanks for wanting to help. I'm really not trying to hurt you, I just have to figure this out myself."

Ava let herself out of the car, and watched him drive off, her anger fading on the heels of his apology. She pulled out her keys and made her way upstairs, more determined than ever to take care of him the best way she knew how.

Inside her apartment, she tossed her purse onto the magnolia-patterned armchair and made her way into the bedroom to her mother's mahogany bureau. The dark metal drawer pulls were cool in her hands as she opened the top drawer. Lifting the red velvet box from its safe place, she felt a thrill as strong as the first time she had held it. But this time it was different, this time she knew what she was doing. Charlotte had trained her well, empowering her to help people overcome life's challenges. Whatever was troubling Ted, Ava could help him, and she would.

She set the case on the rectangular coffee table bearing a thin coating of dust, and took a seat on the floor beside it. Cross-legged, she swiped at the dust with her finger, feeling mildly guilty and neglectful. Housekeeping hadn't exactly been a priority of late. Too many distractions -- chief among them, Ted. Remembering why she was there, Ava shook her head free of all thoughts but one, and opened the box.

"Hello, Beautiful." She took hold of the beaded fob and coaxed the pendulum from its satin nest. "We've got some work to do, for my friend Ted."

Hanging heavy on its silver chain, the rose quartz sphere swayed gently in seeming agreement. Ava breathed deeply. Briefly, she thought of Mary Jane and Casey, each one indebted to Ava for guiding them through rough patches. And they were not alone; not a day went by it seemed without someone seeking help from Ava and the pendulum. Today, that person was Ted, even if he was too stubborn to admit it.

Holding the pendulum still in her hand, Ava skipped the formalities and got straight to the point of asking the question she knew needed to be asked. "Can he fix this on his own?"

More than anything, she wanted to help Ted through whatever "this" was. The stress was crippling him, changing him in ways that Ava did not like; their last conversation was still fresh in her mind. She glanced at the pendulum, already certain of its answer. Swinging ever so slightly to the right, it concurred with her thinking: *No.*

"No surprise there," she muttered to herself, deciding to ask again, for Ted's sake. "Can I help him?"

Ava watched the quartz sphere closely, eager for it to answer her, but the pendulum did not move. After a few moments, she repeated the question, firmly this time. "Can I help him?" Once again, the pendulum remained still.

Frustrated, she placed the pendulum in the palm of her hand. *God damn it, why isn't it working?* Taking a minute to refocus her thoughts, she held it in front of her heart, again. "I'm going to ask you one more time. Can I help Ted?" Still, the pendulum refused to move. Disgusted, she placed it back in its case, the red velvet lid soft in her hands as she secured the cover in place. "Screw it! I already know the answer."

In the darkness of her living room, she considered what to do next. Should she talk to Ted? The pendulum had confirmed that he could not fix things on his own, and even though it had not said anything else, as Ted's best friend, Ava knew she had to help him. She had sound advice for him if she could get him to take it. She doubted he would listen to the pendulum, but maybe he would listen to her.

Getting ready for bed, she thought, "I'll tell him tomorrow."

CHAPTER 19

Dawn arrived with the sound of early morning delivery trucks ambling down Palm Street. Climbing out of bed, Ava dressed in her usual uniform of jeans and a t-shirt and headed to the kitchen to make breakfast. A leftover blueberry muffin and a fresh cup of coffee suited her mood this morning and she sliced the muffin in half, slathering it with butter.

Once seated at the small kitchen table, she thought about last night's session with the pendulum. Although it had not given her all the answers she wanted, she wasn't worried. She knew what to do. She would help Ted get out of his rut and back onto a smoother course.

Finishing her breakfast, she rinsed her dishes in the sink and lifted the shade on the kitchen window. Sun streamed in to flood the small area. It was another beautiful day. A good sign. Grabbing her keys and her purse, she went downstairs to open The Tea Cozy.

Just after seven, Ted walked through the door, his subdued mood a somber version of yesterday as he approached the counter with downcast eyes. Ava noted the change.

"Hey, you," she said. "Thanks again for last night. I had a great time." She paused. "And I'm sorry I upset you talking about Charlie and everything."

Ted looked tired, but he smiled, accepting her apology.

"How are you feeling today?" she asked.

His grandfather's ring clinked against the glass counter top as Ted leaned against it for support. "Last night was rough," he admitted. "Either I couldn't sleep, or I kept waking up when I did."

He rubbed the fatigue from his eyes and looked at Ava. "I've been trying to figure out how I ended up in this mess. Somehow it all just spun out of control."

His eyes met hers. "I'm not a bad person, Ava."

Where did that come from? She stared at him in disbelief, wondering. Stress about work was one thing, but this was crazy. "Of course you're not a bad person. Who said that?" She squeezed his arm for reassurance. "You're smart, accomplished, and kind. You're the best."

"Yeah, I thought I was pretty smart too, but lately that's been debatable."

He was not making any sense, so Ava took a different tact. She covered Ted's hand with hers. "What's going on? Tell me."

"I can't." Tears welled in Ted's eyes. "I wish I could, but I can't."

She could not stand seeing him like this. "Okay, listen to me." Ava's voice was calm but firm, daring him to challenge her. "I know you don't want me involved, but that ship has sailed. You're my friend and I love you. Whatever you're going through, we're in it together. I'm going to help you."

Expecting him to object, Ava hesitated, willing him to grab the lifeline she was throwing him. "Do you understand what I'm saying?" she asked him like he was a young child.

Ted nodded, resigned. "At this point, I'm open to anything you've got."

With the all clear from Ted, Ava charged forward. "I consulted the pendulum last night after you dropped me off. Its message was very clear. I asked several times, to be sure." Ava skipped over the part where the pendulum had not responded.

Speaking with conviction she said, "You absolutely cannot fix the situation by yourself, but with help from your friends everything will be okay. I promise."

"I don't think so, it's pretty complicated."

Ava shook her head. "Listen. I know what I'm talking about. And you know I'm right."

She came around the counter and hugged him. "Please talk to Charlie. He'll listen. He'll know what to do. And he'll understand. I'm sure of it."

Holding her tightly, Ted returned Ava's hug trying to absorb some of her optimism. "We're all human. Everybody makes mistakes, right?" Hope crept into his voice.

Ava smiled, gently cradling Ted's face in her hands. "Right."

Standing tall, he forced himself to smile back. "Thanks for the pep talk, Coach. Guess I better get going."

Another quick hug and he was gone. Ava watched him leave before turning to check on the coffee machines. They both had a busy day ahead of them.

CHAPTER 20

Consumed with dread, Ted walked the short distance to Harper Technologies. Ava was right. He needed to talk to Charlie, but just thinking about it made him sick to his stomach. It would take a saint to forgive him for what he had done, or unconditional love, maybe. Charlie's claim to love him like a son was about to be tested.

He made his way to Charlie's office, fear clinging to every heavy step. Forcing himself forward, he came to a standstill just outside the office door. It was slightly ajar, and Ted could hear Charlie speaking on the phone.

"Really? You're sure? Okay. And you've checked the

numbers several times?" Charlie listened quietly. "How much is missing?"

Ted's knees buckled, bile rising in his throat as his brain tried to process what he had heard. *It's over.* His emotions were fluid moving him through feelings of fear, guilt, and for a brief moment, relief; his secret wasn't a secret anymore. He turned sharply on his heel, walking then running until he was out of the building. He jumped into his car parked next to Charlie's, and with shaking hands slipped the key into the ignition. Gunning the car to the exit, he stopped short of the busy street in front of him. AC blew cool in the car, but Ted was hot, and his neatly pressed collar was damp with sweat.

Charlie knew. It was all he could think about given the conversation he had just overheard. No chance now to come clean and confess or ask for help. That door of opportunity was slammed shut. Charlie knew before Ted could tell him.

Without thought, he took a hard right out of the parking lot, cutting off traffic. Waving his apologies to the angry drivers laying on their horns, he drove aimlessly, his thoughts as confused as his direction, before stopping in front of the post office. In the parked car, Ted slumped over the steering wheel. He was a criminal. He knew it. Charlie knew it. Soon, his family and friends would know it, too. His career was gone with his reputation nipping at its heels. How the hell did he get here?

Thinking back, he remembered going to The Tea Cozy and meeting Ava for the first time. She would probably say it was more than coincidence that brought them together that day; he was just paying off a bet he'd made with the guys in the engineering department. They were friendly wagers on college football games, harmless fun with people at the office. Ted won almost as often as he lost, but even losing was painless when all he had to do was pony up for some of Ava's scones.

What he had not counted on were the wins. They felt so good, like scratching an itch. Every time he won, he wanted to do it again and again. It was easy, since most of the guys just bet on their alma maters. All he had to do was pick the right team and enjoy the winnings. Amateur hour he called it, and it got boring quickly. The day he discovered professional gambling, where money was king and debt a constant threat, was when his troubles began.

He never thought of himself as an addict. He wanted to be a risk taker, like Grandpa Clyde. But in hindsight, an addict is what he became -- addicted to the thrill and the high stakes danger. When he started losing more than winning, he was not deterred. Even when he began dipping into his savings, he was convinced his luck would change. He would bet on it.

The losses continued to mount, eating into his savings until he was broke. But it was College Bowl season, and there was a lot of money to be made for those in the know. He already had the winning teams picked out; he just needed front money to make it happen. He considered asking Susannah or his parents for a short-term loan, before thinking better of it. They would not understand or approve. Out of options, he contacted the friend of a friend. Boone was a bookie. Ted had shuddered at the word and all it inferred but accepted a healthy loan anyway to bankroll his next wager.

"I just need one loan," he had told Boone, not sure why he felt the need to explain himself. "I've been on a bad streak lately, but I've got a good feeling about this game, you know?"

"Whatever." Boone was only interested in one thing. "You've got till Wednesday to pay it back, with interest. Don't be late."

Not one of Ted's chosen teams had won their Bowl game, and he panicked. What the hell did he do now? How was he going to pay Boone back? Again, he considered going to his family, rejecting the idea almost immediately. He could not handle their disappointment. Besides, they would want to know what he was doing, how he could be so reckless; questions even he could not answer.

As Wednesday drew near, Ted was sleepless, wondering and worrying about how he was going to pay Boone back. As he saw it, there was only one way out. The next morning, before anyone else got there, he had slipped quietly into the office. From his desk, he worked quickly, fingers flying as he logged into the company financial statements. It did not take long to create a bogus client and transfer funds disguised as a payable invoice to the new account. He authorized a wire transfer and prepared to send $10,000 of the company's money into his personal account. His finger shook as it pressed the computer key, completing the unscrupulous task. It was just a loan, and he would pay it back in full, as soon as he had a win.

But the win was elusive, seemingly always just out of reach, and the loan he borrowed became multiple loans as he worked to pay back his debts. Ted took frequent sums of money from the company coffers to satisfy Boone, but the bookie had grown more persistent and dangerous, calling Ted at work, where Charlie might overhear. He wanted so badly to hate him, but he wasn't the one who stole $100,000 from his employer. The truth was, Ted hated himself.

Now that Charlie knew the truth, it was only a matter of time before his family and the rest of Wicks Falls learned the truth, too. He glanced at the clock tower, wondering how long before the police came looking for him. How long before Charlie turned him in? Reaching into the glove compartment, Ted pulled out a small writing pad and pen. His first letter was to his boss. He wondered when and where they would see each other again. Court was no place to have a private conversation, and face-to-face, Ted doubted he would have the courage to say what he really wanted to. It was too hard, if Charlie would even listen. Better to put it on paper. That was real, and forever. Maybe some day, Charlie would understand the mistakes he'd made, and forgive him.

The words flowed from his pen, succinct and sincere. There was really only one way to apologize; sorry was such a small word, but it was the best Ted could do. Charlie wouldn't care that he was sick with shame, his heart broken by what he had done, or that he was disgusted with his own reflection in the rearview mirror. Only one thing would matter to Charlie: why? Ted wished he knew.

Maybe it was the siren call of bigger risk, greater gain that caught hold of him. The indescribable rush when he won, the money, and the heady power of accurately predicting something before it happened. The problem was he did not win enough. Scratch that. The problem was, he could not stop trying. Win or lose, nothing made him feel more alive. Whatever it took, he would do it, he explained in a second letter to his parents and Susannah; no one and nothing else mattered more.

Ted's stressed body ached with fear and fatigue. His hands gripped the steering wheel, supporting him as he stared at his grandfather's ring. The hematite crystal was mesmerizing, gleaming hard and black, and a calm settled upon him just like Ava had said. Retrieving the pad and pen from the passenger seat beside him, he quickly scribbled another message, this time to Ava. It killed him to think about her knowing. What would she think of him? That he was a liar? Maybe. That he was a loser? Absolutely.

Ted forced himself out of the car and up the steep flight of stairs into the post office. Cool air embraced him, comforting him as he waited in line to buy envelopes and stamps. At this hour, the post office was quiet, and the short line moved quickly. He walked purposefully to a long marble counter with pens anchored by beaded metal chains and started addressing the envelopes. Within minutes, they were signed, sealed, and stamped, and he dropped the letters into the mail slot.

The late morning sun was blinding as he stepped out of the post office. Raising his hand, he shielded his eyes, letting them adjust to the brilliance of the day, before making his way to the car. The only ones left to speak with now were the police. Turning the key in the ignition, the car purred to life as he pulled out of the parking spot. Ted's mind was blank as he drove defenseless against the anxiety that overwhelmed him. There had to be another way. Turning the car around, he headed for home.

Half expecting a driveway full of cars with flashing red and blue lights, he was relieved to find it quiet when he pulled into his garage. Ted tried to calm himself, but he knew the storm was coming. It was inevitable. The car idled, waiting for him to decide what to do. Should he run? He glanced at the dashboard; the fuel tank was full. The headrest cushioned him as he leaned against it, tired and resigned. Running was not an option any more than staying was. Facing Charlie and his family with what he had done was going to kill them. Silently, he reclined his seat; closing his eyes, he pressed the garage door closed.

CHAPTER 21

Monday morning came swiftly; Ava barely remembered what she had done over the weekend. After working part of both days, she had filled the rest of her time with errands and busy work. On Sundays, she tried to save a few hours for reading. Yesterday's choice, *Shopping for Love*, showed great potential through the first six chapters. It was just the kind of temporary, lighthearted escape that she loved.

She hurried down her apartment stairs, reaching in her front skirt pocket for the keys to The Tea Cozy. She grabbed the neatly tied pile of newspapers waiting for her on the door's threshold. The *Wicks Falls Courant* proudly touted itself as South Carolina's third oldest daily paper and purveyor of "hard news and investigative reporting." Ava chuckled at the thought of any hard news in Wicks Falls, save for the occasional theft or domestic dispute. Readers were more likely to find articles about the Wicks Falls Wildcats football team, recipes, maybe some gossip, and on Thursdays, the weekend events calendar.

As she slipped her key into the lock, Ava glanced down at the front page. *"LOCAL BUSINESSMAN COMMITS"* commanded the fold, but Ava could not see the rest of the headline until she untied the stack. "Uh oh," she thought. "I bet someone got caught driving after a few too many cocktails." Ava shook her head trying to imagine who had screwed up this time.

Inside, she released the papers from the tie, unfolding the front page for a closer look. Her eyes grew wide, her knees nearly buckling as she read the news. Grabbing the edge of a nearby table to steady herself, she held her hand over her mouth to keep the contents of her breakfast from resurfacing.

"No!" she screamed. "Oh God, no!" Scanning the article, Ava searched frantically for answers.

"LOCAL BUSINESSMAN COMMITS SUICIDE? FUNDS MISSING."

A picture of Ted smiled at her from the center of the page. Her Ted -- her handsome, successful, oatmeal raisin cookie-loving, no fan of the pendulum Ted.

Monday, June 29 – *Theodore Andrew Miller, 34, of 17 Wind Whistle Drive, was discovered dead on Friday of apparent carbon monoxide poisoning in the garage of his home. Neighbors alerted police to the sound of a running motor late Friday afternoon. With the assistance of the Wicks Falls fire department, police entered the garage to find Miller slumped over the wheel of his vehicle. Medical personnel pronounced him dead at the scene. While the investigation is ongoing, no foul play is suspected at this time. The family has been notified.*

Police added that Mr. Miller's death coincided with a recent investigation by South Carolina State Police into missing funds from his employer, Harper Technologies. The investigation is ongoing. No charges have been filed.

Ava's head throbbed with panic and pain. Unable to reach a chair, she sank to the floor. *Why?* She was so confused. She was sure Ted had left The Tea Cozy ready to turn things around. She told him he could not do it on his own, that he needed to talk to Charlie, and he had agreed.

Charlie. Ava glanced back at the article, rereading ". . . *missing funds from his employer, Harper Technologies.*" What missing funds? When Ted told her he'd messed up she'd thought he was referring to his work. Was there more to it? Was he stealing money from Harper?

"No!" Still slumped on the floor, Ava argued with herself. "Ted would never steal money. And he certainly wouldn't steal money from Charlie."

Then what? Pulling herself up slowly from the floor, she reached into her handbag for her cell phone.

Her fingers dialed clumsily. "Hey, Casey," she whispered hoarsely into the phone.

"Ava?" Casey replied. "Are you okay? Why are you whispering?"

"Can you come in to work now? I need your help right away. There's been a terrible tragedy and I don't think I can handle customers all by myself this morning."

"What happened?" Casey asked, alarmed.

Ava took a deep breath but still could only whisper. "It's Ted, Casey. He's dead."

"Dead?" Casey shrieked in disbelief. "What are you talking about?"

Ignoring Casey's question, Ava asked again, "Can you come?"

"Hold on, Ava. I'll be there in half an hour."

When Casey arrived, the two women hugged, crying as they held onto to each other. Finally, Ava picked up a newspaper and showed Casey the article. "What do they mean they're investigating missing funds? Do you think Ted stole money from Harper? Why would he need to steal money? He had a good job there." Casey fired the questions at Ava.

A subdued Ava answered her quietly. "I don't know any more than you do, Casey. I can't imagine why Ted would steal money. It doesn't make any sense." Her voice trailed off.

"Why don't you go upstairs and rest?" Casey soothed,

gently rubbing Ava's back. "I can handle the morning crowd. I'm sure the news is spreading like wildfire and you don't need to be around for that."

"I can't. I wouldn't know what to do with myself upstairs. I'd go crazy staring at the walls." Ava was firm. "If someone knows something, I want to be here to hear it."

"I get it. Whatever you need. Just let me know." Casey reached for her apron.

Feeling like she'd been hit by a tractor-trailer, Ava washed her face with cold water from the kitchen sink. The morning crept by, one slow and painful minute at a time. As Casey predicted, most of the customers had read the morning paper and rumors were already swirling around Wicks Falls and in The Tea Cozy.

"I heard he was in debt, over his head. Charlie never saw it coming. Supposedly, he left Harper in a tough spot," Beau Chalmers announced as he picked up his decaffeinated coffee and blueberry scone from the counter.

"There were people coming and going at his house for the last several months. I saw them with my own eyes. I'm betting on drugs. Dealing maybe," Deb Mortimore added.

Ava's heart broke a shard at a time with each comment. The community she loved, that Ted loved, was tearing his character apart piece by piece. And none of it was true; it couldn't be. Her Ted would never do something like that. "Ted is not a drug dealer, Deb. He is honest to a fault." Speaking in the present tense, Ava bit her quivering lip. "He was." She wiped the already clean counter for distraction.

"He was a good man."

He was a man who had needed her help. That much Ava knew, and she had let him down. She should have listened more, asked more questions, pressed for details when Ted told her he was in trouble. But she was so sure she had all the answers.

Charlotte. Ava thought about her spiritual mentor. How many times had Charlotte warned her not to insert her ego when she consulted the pendulum? "Ask the questions," Charlotte had said. "Pass along the answers as they're given. Don't confuse either with your own advice." She could only imagine what Charlotte would say when she discovered Ava's role in Ted's death. The pendulum had not been willing to give her an answer, and Ava should have heeded its pause. Instead, she charged ahead, confident that she could help him.

Casey enveloped her in a big bear hug as Ava's spirit continued to wilt. "Ava, please don't listen to the gossip. Ted was a wonderful person. Let's wait until the police finish their investigation before we jump to conclusions."

"Oh, Casey." Ava's guilt brought fresh tears to her eyes. "I saw Ted last week. I literally bumped into him on the street. He was upset and distracted, but he wouldn't tell me what was wrong. I thought he was just stressed from working so much. Then driving home from dinner at Charlie Harper's house, we had an argument. The poor guy has been in such a bad way for a while now. I just wanted to help. I consulted the pendulum and the next day when he came to The Tea Cozy, I told him what he needed to do."

Casey was sympathetic. "It's okay, Honey."

"No, Casey. I've been thinking about it all morning. I didn't do it right. I didn't respect the process. Charlotte warned me. My job was to relay the message, not to insert myself. But I did everything she told me not to do."

Ava glanced nervously around making sure no one could overhear her. "Casey, this is my fault. I told Ted he couldn't do it himself. I insisted that he talk to Charlie. I told him that I'm never wrong. And the worst part is it had nothing to do with the pendulum. It wouldn't even answer my questions." Her eyes dropped to the floor, shame creeping over her face. "He did this because of me."

Tinkling bells above The Tea Cozy door announced another customer. Ava rushed to the kitchen, not wanting anyone to see her upset.

"Hi, Rory. Got anything good in there today?" Casey gestured towards the pile of mail that Rory Porter was delivering.

Rory, all tanned face and sparkling green eyes, handed Casey the day's mail and quipped, "Just the usual, bills and advertisements. Oh, and there's this, too." He gave Casey an envelope addressed to Ava.

"Thanks, Rory."

"What do you think of the Ted Miller news?" Rory blurted, watching closely for Casey's reaction.

"Don't you start making assumptions like everybody else in this town," Casey lectured. "Ted was a good guy and we don't know what happened. Let the police figure it out and then we can all have an opinion."

Rory pursed his lips. "Okay. You're right. I've heard a lot of talk on my delivery route today, but no one really knows anything for sure."

"Well, you might want to remind people to think about Ted's family. They must be devastated," Casey fumed.

Rory nodded. "True. Susannah must be destroyed. She and Ted were so close." He headed towards the door. "Okay, you're right; I'll keep my opinion to myself for now." Giving Casey a quick wave, he adjusted his mailbag and left.

Clutching the mail pile, Casey followed Rory to the door and turned the "OPEN" sign over to its "CLOSED" counterpart, locking the door for good measure. She did not want to hear any more opinions about what caused the demise of Ted Miller today. Tomorrow, hopefully, the good people of Wicks Falls would be more thoughtful about honoring Ted and his family. She sighed. Death was never easy, but it was clear that Ted's death was complicated and people were going to demand the truth, however ugly it might be.

Back in the kitchen, Ava looked completely broken. Casey handed her the mail. "I just closed up. It's almost dinnertime anyway. Please go upstairs and relax. You did NOT cause this. Whatever was going on with Ted was his to own. They were his demons, honey. Promise me you'll just take it easy and we'll tackle tomorrow as a new day."

Ava nodded numbly. "Casey, what would I do without

you?"

Casey hugged her again. "We'll get through this together. I'm going home to feed Gordie now, but I'm here if you need me. Promise you'll call if you want to talk."

"I promise." Ava spoke so softly, Casey strained to hear her.

"Okay. See you in the morning." Casey grabbed her handbag and headed for the door. She turned and blew Ava a kiss. "Love you."

Ava turned off the lights and locked The Tea Cozy's door behind her before heading upstairs to her apartment. Once inside, she lowered herself gingerly onto the couch, still clutching the day's mail in her hands, the envelope resting on the top of the pile. Puzzled, she felt a lump through the paper. It was small, about the size of a marble.

The envelope ripped easily as Ava pulled a folded piece of paper from inside, and the lump tumbled into her lap. It only took her a second to realize what it was: Grandpa Clyde's ring. Filled with dread, she opened the paper slowly.

Ava,

I didn't get to Charlie in time, but I wanted you to know that at least I tried. I should never have doubted you and your pendulum. Maybe if I'd listened to you sooner this wouldn't have happened. I'm sending you my grandfather's ring for safekeeping. You're more worthy of it than I'll ever be. I am so sorry.

Ted

Ava was sick to her stomach. She still had no idea what the Harper investigation was about or how Ted was involved, but it didn't matter. Ted was gone. She read the note again, picturing him writing it as she did. *I should never have doubted you and your pendulum.*

There was just one problem; the pendulum had not given her any advice. Its stubborn refusal to answer was a message in itself, one she had deliberately ignored and in so doing failed the one person who mattered most. She had spent the past year dispensing advice to anyone who would listen until they believed in her gift as much as she did. She was such a fool. Charlotte had said Wicked Wednesdays were nothing more than pure entertainment and had warned her about using the pendulum in such a public way. But Ava had been too fixated on the attention they brought her. Now, her careless ways had finally caught up to her.

Ava stood, putting Grandpa Clyde's ring into the pocket of her shorts. She needed some guidance. Pushing away her guilty thoughts, she looked for the red velvet box. It was on the kitchen table where she'd left it open to allow the day's sun to shine its cleansing energy on the pendulum. Returning to the sofa, Ava sat and held it in front of her heart. She tried to take a deep breath, but it got hung up in her lungs, jagged, painful, and full of remorse. She tried again with a shallow breath, focusing solely on the pink quartz. It was time for her to put her money where her mouth was; she hoped the pendulum would forgive her and tell her what she had to do.

It was almost impossible for her to calm her nerves, but she had to make sure her hand was steady. "I'm putting it out to the universe. I respectfully call on all higher powers to help me find clarity." There was no way she would forget to start with a prayer, not this time.

The pink sphere was motionless. "What should I do about Ted?" Ava asked and then chided herself. *For Christ's sake, Ava, be specific and focus on what you want to know.*

Pausing to reframe her thoughts, Ava tried again. "Did Ted take his own life?" She needed to understand if the rumors that had spiraled today around The Tea Cozy like a cyclone were true. The pendulum moved definitively to the left. *Yes.* Ava bit her lip to keep her tears away. She could not imagine how desperate and alone Ted must have been felt.

"Did Ted need my help?" She wanted to know if her original intentions were in the right place. Once again, the pendulum swung to the left. *Yes.*

"Okay. Now we're getting somewhere," Ava affirmed, surprised that the pendulum had answered the question, unlike the day before. *But why?* She had no answer but could not dwell on that now. Instead, she considered the rumor that Ted had stolen from Charlie. It seemed impossible, but could it have pushed him to the brink? She needed to know if her interference had made things worse for Ted.

"He needed my help, but I didn't ask how. Did I make things worse?" She needed to know. *Yes.* The pendulum's slow swing was an accusation. Guilty as charged. Ava let go of the pendulum and covered her face with her hands.

This time she would respect what the pendulum said. It was clear; Ted had taken his own life, and she had made his situation worse. Both she and the pendulum knew why; this one was on her. Ava panicked. She had to leave, and right away.

She scratched out a quick note to Casey, before going to her bedroom and pulling two suitcases from the closet. Without thinking, Ava loaded clothes and shoes haphazardly into the nylon luggage. She cleared the bathroom countertop of her cosmetic essentials and shoved them into a plastic bag. Moving to the kitchen, she grabbed a cooler from her small pantry and filled it with items from her refrigerator: water bottles, milk, a few containers of yogurt, and a block of Havarti cheese. She grabbed a loaf of bread and some bananas from the counter and added them to the cooler.

A half hour later, the bags and cooler were sitting in a disorganized pile at the bottom of the stairs. Ava dragged herself to the top for a final check of the apartment where everything was neat, tidy, and in its place. She turned the lights off, closing and locking the door behind her, and returned to the pile of bags below. One by one, she loaded them into the car.

At length, she approached the door of The Tea Cozy standing in front of it like it was a mirror. Her reflection looked small in the glass, her guilt disguised in a pair of cotton shorts and an oversized t-shirt. Reaching into her back pocket, she pulled out the note for Casey. "I'm sorry, my friend." She slipped it through the old-fashioned mail slot, rarely used since Rory had started delivering the mail and turned away.

Sully Shores

CHAPTER 22

Close to midnight, the headlights of Ava's car found the family cottage. She pulled through the driftwood markers near the road, her tires crunching over the crushed shells as she opened the car window and breathed in the salt air. Even in darkness, there was something so distinct about that smell. Ava followed the driveway to the front of the cottage and parked. With the help of a small sliver of moonlight, she could just make out the porch, large enough for two plastic beach chairs and a small table holding a mishmash of shells abandoned long ago by their inhabitants.

Above the front door a homemade sign, faded and worn, welcomed her back to "Sea Glass Manor." It matched the "CGLSMNR" license plate she had sported on her car since she first got her driver's license many years ago. The sign had been Mary's idea.

"Let's name the cottage," she announced one day as they lounged lazily on beach towels.

"Name the cottage? What do you mean?" little Ava asked.

Mary thought aloud. "We can name the house something that is meaningful to the three of us. It will give it a swankiness."

"What's swankiness?"

"It's a specialness, I guess," Mary answered. "It will make the cottage sound important if we name it. And it certainly is important to us."

David had just laughed. "Mary, you do realize we're talking about a small five-room cottage, right? I'm not sure anyone would call it swanky."

Mary swatted him on the arm. "David, our little slice of paradise is going to have a name, and it has to be perfect." She raised her eyebrows at both of them.

Summer had nearly passed before they came up with it. Mary dismissed several suggestions as too silly, too serious, or not quite swanky enough. Finally, during one of their daily walks along the shore, with their feet splashing in the sandy water of breaking waves, she made up her mind.

"That's it!" she declared, as David unearthed a piece of brown glass tumbled smooth by the ocean from beneath a clamshell.

"What's it? This?" David asked, pointing to the tiny fragment.

"Yes!" Mary's enthusiasm was contagious.

"We're finally getting a name." David winked at Ava who giggled. "It's not going to be 'Brown Beer Bottle Bed and Breakfast' is it?" he asked.

"David!" Mary chastised him. "No. I think we should call it 'Sea Glass Manor.' It has a dignified sound to it."

Ava repeated the name to herself. "I love it, Mom. It's perfect."

David considered the moniker for a moment before agreeing. "Sea Glass Manor it is. We'll make a sign and hang it over the front door."

All these years later, those memories filled Ava's head, along with another, more painful one. Closing her eyes, she saw herself and her dad sitting on the small front porch. Ava was slurping a cherry Popsicle, her favorite, trying to ward off the mid-day heat, and David sat beside her with a small white box in his lap.

"What's that, Dad?"

"It's something I had made, just for you," he told her. "When you wear it, I hope it reminds you of all our favorite things."

"Hold out your hand and close your eyes," he instructed and Ava dutifully obeyed. Putting her frozen treat on the table, she uncurled her small fingers, only half closing her eyes.

"You're peeking!" he scolded, covering them with his hand. Ava laughed.

"Dad, stop! What is it?" She tried to push his hand away.

"Okay, okay, I'll tell you. You know, we've made some pretty wonderful memories here." He uncovered her eyes. "This is for you, so you always remember how happy we are here."

Her father was holding the most beautiful piece of sea glass she had ever seen, an exquisite mix of blue and green, like the ocean. Its smooth surface was entwined in polished silver wire as bright as the silver chain he fastened around her neck.

"Dad, it's beautiful," she sighed, staring down at it. "Where did you find it?"

"Remember when we walked down to Halsey Pier a few weeks ago? I saw it on the sand, tangled in some seaweed. I swear it's the prettiest piece of glass I've ever found, and I wanted my beautiful girl to have it."

David hugged Ava. "Think of me and your mom when you wear it, Honey. We'll always be with you."

A few weeks later, her dad was dead, killed in a single car accident. Mary did her best to comfort her daughter while mourning her husband, but Ava had never really gotten over losing him. She wore David's necklace every day, touching the glass for comfort.

Pushing her memories aside, Ava began emptying the contents of the car. She grabbed the last of the bags and bundles, remnants of her Wicks Falls life, and brought them inside dropping them in an unceremonious heap on the floor. She looked around, noting the shabby chairs and tables and the old blue sofa that had been there forever. Mary had always insisted that it was more than just a house; it was a home. With a sigh, she left everything where it was on the floor. Too tired to do anything but sleep, she made her way into the bedroom and crawled under the covers of her childhood bed.

The next morning the sheets felt hot against Ava's skin as she rolled over. Each time she had tossed and turned during the night, they had wrapped tighter and tighter around her until she felt like a caterpillar in a cocoon. Opening her eyes, she extracted herself from the covers and stared at the ceiling. A crusty residue lined the edges of her eyelashes, the dried remains of many tears falling throughout the night. Slowly, she swung her legs over the side of the bed, feeling for her slippers on the floor. Pulling on a light zip-up hoodie, she walked the short distance to the tiny kitchen.

The old coffee pot sat on the stove, its silver metal sides scratched from years of use. Ava's movements were automated as she prepared a small cup of coffee and sliced a bagel, slathering it with cream cheese. She had missed dinner the night before, and suddenly, she was starving. Thankful she had brought food with her, Ava devoured every last bite.

Her meal finished, she wandered into the living room and noted the rest of her things still sitting where she had left them on the floor. "Nope. I'm not dealing with you yet."

Shaking her head, she returned to the bedroom to throw on a
t-shirt and her shorts from the night before. Ava grabbed a
baseball hat from the closet to shade her face and turned to
go. As she shoved her hands deep into her pockets, her
fingers made contact with the metal of Grandpa Clyde's ring.
She had put it there for safekeeping, but now she wanted it
gone. *I just can't go there right now.* Tossing it on the dresser like
a hot potato she hurried outside to the welcoming beach.

It was a typical day for Sully Shores -- the sun was strong
and bright and there was a slight breeze that made the sea
grasses dance as they guarded the dunes. High in the sky,
dozens of seagulls called to each other. When Ava was a little
girl, she used to love watching them swoop into the water
from up above and come away with a clamshell hanging from
their mouths. They would drop the clams on the rocks below
to crack open their shells, then scoop the fresh meat into
their beaks. She had felt bad for the defenseless clams, but
David always said it was nature's way. Today was no
different; she watched as they worked on securing their lunch.

A few steps out, Ava took a look back at the cottage. In
the daylight, she was reminded how charming the place really
was, built in the 1950's in true coastal cottage style with
weathered shingles and white trim. Rose bushes, planted
almost twenty years ago, formed a privacy hedge around the
house. Roses were one of Mary's favorites and beach roses
were exceptional; the flower appeared so beautiful and
delicate, but in reality, it was a hardy plant. An old outdoor
shower was off to the side and Ava smiled remembering her
mother's insistence that sandy feet be washed before coming
inside.

She walked to the shore, submerging her toes into the cool relief of the sea, and watched the foamy waves bubble around her ankles before heading south, towards Halsey Pier. The pier would no doubt be busy; it was a favorite spot for fishermen to cast their long lines into the waves, while hungry birds circled above squawking and looking for scraps of fish left on the long wooden planks.

She strolled down the beach, the sand not yet hot beneath her feet, carefully keeping her mind blank; thinking would only lead to dark thoughts. That was why she had come here after all, to escape. She knew she could not avoid her fears and doubts forever. Eventually she would have to confront them, but not yet, and not now.

Sidestepping a piece of driftwood stuck in her sandy path, Ava's gaze shifted as she caught sight of a woman just a few yards away. She was a beach painter. That is what Mary and David had called the artists who set up their easels and small stools on the sand, their paints tucked into a box at their feet, trying to capture the right light and mood for the perfect seascape. In the winter especially, dozens of them lined the shore each day, all of them painting the same view.

This woman was no different; her easel rested on a stand as she painted from her stool, a palette of acrylics in her hand. Ava could not make out the canvas but assumed it was another Sully Shores' seascape. She slowed as she passed, surprised to see that she was wrong. It was a non-descript house surrounded by beautiful gardens.

The woman glanced up from her painting. With a nod, she acknowledged Ava examining her work. Ava blushed, feeling caught like a peeping Tom. Speaking of houses, it was time to get back to hers.

CHAPTER 23

The ocean breeze settled gently between Ava's shoulders, giving her a gentle push as she climbed the last few steps to the cottage. Grasping the front door handle, she turned to look once more at the vast expanse of curling waves crashing on shore. They seemed to be begging her to come back and play. "Later," she murmured, reluctantly entering the house.

With hands on hips, Ava took stock of the living room floor. Her eyes twitched at the chaotic sight of suitcases, bags, and boxes haphazardly strewn across the sun-bleached hardwoods. The messy remnants of her midnight flight from Wicks Falls were a blatant reminder of why she was here. It was hardly her proudest moment. Running away from home was a cowardly thing to do. With a heavy sigh, she grabbed the suitcases and carried them into her bedroom.

Long ago, Ava's mother had established a routine that became a tradition of the Dell family's visits to Sully Shores. "Chores first," Mary would say, "and fun always." It was a refrain she had repeated to Ava from a very early age, along with "many hands make light work." Ava smiled, remembering how excited she would be as their car pulled into the driveway. "We're here!" she would shriek, throwing off her seat belt as she raced for the cottage with her parents at her heels.

Their tasks were always the same. David emptied the car of their belongings, making countless trips back and forth until everything was inside. Mary was in charge of the kitchen, stocking the cupboards and refrigerator before putting fresh linens on the beds and towels in the bathroom. Ava was the sweeper using her trusty broom Sandy to clean the cottage floors and the front porch.

Holding Sandy now, Ava tried to remember the last time she had been here. *Too long,* she thought, gripping the wooden handle in her hands as she swept each room clean, opening the shutters and windows, and inviting the fresh air in as she went. It felt strange to be here alone without her parents; just thinking about it made her sad.

Finally, after a few hours of scrubbing and scouring, she was ready to call it quits. The cottage seemed to glow from her ministrations. The old wood furniture gleamed bright as new. Daylight streamed through freshly washed windows that sparkled like crystals. Breathing deeply, Ava filled her lungs with lemon-scented air and looked around. The house was spotless. There was only one more thing left to do.

Throwing a towel over her shoulder, she made her way outside to her favorite part of Sea Glass Manor. The paneled outdoor shower had always been a haven to her. As a little girl she had giggled with delight at not bathing inside; as a dreamy-eyed teenager, she had spent hours under the shower's spray thinking about boys and Brad Pitt, her celebrity crush. But today, she was here for a little TLC.

The hot and cold faucets squeaked to life in her hands as she adjusted the temperature, steam forming as the water sprayed forcefully from the oversized showerhead. Leaving her clothes on the built-in bench, Ava moved under the water and lifted her face to the sky. Warm rain poured down on her, soothing, cleansing. Beneath the water's gentle kneading her tense muscles uncoiled and Ava sighed with pleasure.

Her nimble fingers moved from memory to the soap dish anchored on the wall. Mary had ended every visit by putting a new bar of soap in the shower. "A promise that we'll be back," she had explained. With silent thanks, Ava unwrapped the soap, turning it in her wet hands to create a foamy lather and bathed away the day's grime and fatigue.

Back in the house, she rummaged through her suitcase for a clean pair of shorts and a t-shirt and put them on. She combed carelessly through her damp hair, fluffing it dry as she twisted it into a messy bun, and started to unpack. The bulging suitcases made her grimace as she sorted through them. She had enough clothes to stay there a lifetime, if she wanted to. She would have to think about that. Reaching into her luggage, she pulled out something soft and square.

The pendulum. Eyeing it warily, she sat deflated on the edge of the bed.

For a few hours at least, she had managed to forget why she was really there. But the pendulum brought it all slamming back. In a speed-packing frenzy, she had moved about her apartment grabbing and tossing her things into disorganized piles. Not knowing what she would need in the days ahead, she had taken everything, including the pendulum. She wanted it with her as a constant reminder of what had happened. Charlotte's beautiful gift had become her curse.

No matter how hard she tried, there was no escaping that fact. Ava curled on her bed in a fetal position. She missed Ted. Closing her eyes, she pictured him in front of her, flashing a smile and a wave as he grabbed his coffee on the run; in her apartment, his fingers tapping impatiently on the table as he waited his turn playing Scrabble; standing at her front door with ice cream, candles, and a sleeping bag during a hurricane, just in case she was scared to be alone.

Now she was alone again without any chance of Ted coming to keep her company. That was the pattern of her life it seemed; the people she loved always left her. She shivered and pulled a warm afghan over her to ward off the emotional chill. As the sun began its descent into night, she closed her eyes. Maybe sleep would be her friend.

CHAPTER 24

A chirping bird roused Ava from her slumber as morning light filled the room with a blinding brightness. She groaned, not yet ready to face a new day, and burrowed deeper into the soft, soothing darkness of her pillow. The bird chirped again, persistent or maybe insistent, piquing her curiosity. Climbing out of bed, Ava padded barefoot into the living room to investigate.

The early morning offender rested on the coffee table where she had abandoned it the day before. Ava's cell phone vibrated noisily with notices of text messages and missed calls that glowed reprimanding on the screen. Except for the short note to Casey, she had left home without a word to anyone.

"Knock it off." She picked up the phone, scowling as if it could hear her and scrolled through her messages: forty-two texts, most of them from Casey, a few from Mary Jane and other friends, all of them concerned for her.

"Where are you, how are you?"

"Here for you."

"Unbelievable news about Ted. Let me know if I can help."

There were only ten voicemail messages. Ava understood why. It was so much harder to speak with someone in crisis than to quietly text your support. She listened as Casey spoke nine times, her voice thick with emotion as she sniffed into the phone: "Oh, Ava. I'm so worried about you. Please take care of yourself and take all the time you need. I've got things under control here. Love you."

Ava's lips curved into a sad smile. She missed Casey, The Tea Cozy, Wicks Falls, and home.

"Ava, are you there? Pick up, please." Charlotte's clipped voice commanded from the final voicemail message.

She hesitated afraid to hear the harsh scolding she knew was coming. Charlotte's warning rang in her ears: *The power is in the pendulum. Never let your personal interests interfere.* She could not have been anymore clear, and yet, Ava had completely contradicted Charlotte's very explicit instructions.

Ava tossed the phone back on the table, ending the call. The stress of it all was too much for her. Massaging her throbbing temples, she startled as the wall clock chimed seven. "I've gotta get out of here," she muttered. Grabbing a light pullover, Ava fled out the door to the beach.

A soft breeze lifted the hair from her face as she walked briskly away from the cottage, the lenient sand giving way beneath her feet with each steadfast step. Seagulls circled high above calling to each other. Ava ignored them, her long strides carrying her farther and farther down the beach. The sea air was healing; it filled her lungs and soothed her senses.

Her steps slowed to a stop as she grew calm, and she sat to rest. A handful of people strolled the beach while a young family searched together for tidal pool treasures. They reminded Ava of her own family and happier times at Sully Shores. The sand vibrated lightly beneath her as she turned her wistful gaze to a lone barefoot runner, ear buds snug in his ears. Rhythmically, he jogged past her, lost in a world of pace and time. She watched him run, putting distance between them, until she was alone once again.

Searching for a distraction, Ava settled upon a beach painter set up a short ways off from where she sat. The woman, in her sixties Ava guessed, wore a long, flowing caftan that moved as one with the ocean breeze, the pink paisley fabric accentuating the color of her cheeks. Her hair was thick and snowy white, pulled back in a low chignon as elegant as the woman herself. She looked familiar. Squinting her eyes for a closer look, Ava recognized the woman from yesterday.

She stood brushing off the sandy seat of her shorts and began walking back to the cottage. She needed breakfast to quiet the rumbling in her stomach. As she passed the beach painter, Ava returned the woman's smile with one of her own. Brilliant hues of color splashed across the woman's canvas depicting a turquoise sea balancing a mandarin sunrise. It was lovely, but typical. Ava wondered if she had finished the other painting, the one of the house. Maybe tomorrow she would ask her about it. Waving shyly to the woman, she broke into a slow trot home.

CHAPTER 25

The Earl Grey tea cascaded out of the carafe into a paper cup, steam rising from the hot liquid. Casey carefully encased it in a cardboard sleeve before handing it to Mary Jane. Stepping from behind the counter, she wiped off the nearby tables with a damp cloth, capturing crumbs leftover from the breakfast crowd, and keeping herself busy.

"Not a word," she said to Mary Jane, shaking her head. "I've called her a thousand times but she's not answering. I've left more than a half a dozen messages."

"I know. I've tried texting her, too. Nothing. Tell me what her note said." Mary Jane blew gently on her tea.

"She said she couldn't stay, that it would be impossible to let everyone know how sorry she was. She feels responsible for Ted's death. She told me it was her fault because she consulted the pendulum and then insisted that Ted follow her advice."

"That's ridiculous," Mary Jane scoffed. "The police are still investigating, and Charlie Harper isn't talking. But I did see Jeff Olsen, he works there, too, and he said that Ted had completely manipulated the company computer system. It'll be weeks before they can make any sense of it all."

She bit into a cinnamon scone, licking the sugar coating from her lips.

"I know." Casey sighed, tossing the damp rag onto the self-service table. "I'm not sure what to do. I mean, I can take care of things here, but I feel so bad for Ava. She thinks she's responsible and she's afraid that Charlotte will too."

Mary Jane nodded. "Does Charlotte know she's gone?"

Casey shrugged her shoulders. "I'm not sure, I haven't seen her. I did call Georgia to see if Ava was with her. She had no idea Ava had left. Then, I had to tell her about Ted, which was awful because Georgia knows how close they were. Now I'm thinking if she didn't go to Georgia's, she must be alone."

"Where do you think she went?" Mary Jane asked. "Sully Shores?"

"Probably. I mean where else would she go?" The front door creaked, letting Casey know they were not alone.

Charlotte stood in the doorframe, dressed in a bright purple gauze tunic with a turquoise studded silver belt.

"Hey there." Casey tried to sound nonchalant.

"Where's Ava?" Charlotte charged, not mincing words for pleasantries. Approaching the women, she dumped her large tote on a nearby table and pulled out her phone, waving it in the air.

"I've called her twice and she hasn't called me back." She placed her hands on her hips and gave Casey a look.

"She's not here right now," Casey stalled. "She went away for a few days."

Charlotte was not satisfied with her answer. "Went where? You don't just pack up and leave in the middle of the night. I'm not an idiot, Casey; I know this must have something to do with Ted. They were so close. It doesn't make sense that she'd leave now."

Casey exchanged a knowing glance with Mary Jane, silently warning her not to say anything.

"I really don't know where she is, Charlotte. I'm still checking in with a couple of her friends to see if anyone's heard from her."

"I don't have a good feeling about this." Charlotte paused to look at the two women. "What the hell is going on around here? This whole Ted mess, things like that just don't happen in Wicks Falls. The papers say he might have embezzled from Charlie's company. Why would he do that? Charlie loved him."

Mary Jane and Casey stood mute.

Exasperated, Charlotte huffed, "Fine. I'll take a blueberry muffin and a cup of decaf tea to go."

"Of course, and don't worry, it's only been a couple of days. I'm sure Ava will turn up. I'll let you know as soon as I hear from her," Casey offered.

With her order ready, Charlotte gathered her things together. "Please do. And just so you know, I'm not completely heartless. Ted was a good person, and I know Ava adored him. This must be tearing her apart."

With a turn on her macramé espadrilles, she left without another word.

"Thank God she's finally gone. But you know she'll be back and then what do we do?" Mary Jane said pursing her lips. "She can get to the truth any number of different ways."

Casey drummed her fingers on the countertop. "Even when I do find out where Ava is, there's no way I'm telling Charlotte. Who knows? Maybe she'll figure it out on her own. We just have to be patient. Ava will call when she's ready."

Mary Jane tipped the paper cup to sip the last remnants of her tea before tossing it into the trash.

"Do you think she'll be back for Ted's funeral? I can't believe she'd miss it."

Casey shook her head, her elbows anchored on the counter. "I'm hoping she just needs a few days to get her head on straight. She'll come back, eventually. She has to."

CHAPTER 26

A kaleidoscope of colors pressed together willy-nilly on the wooden pallet: blues, beiges, oranges, and yellows all waiting patiently to be used. The artist dipped her paintbrush into the Persian blue and swept the soft bristles over the canvas in long, broad strokes. It was the start of a Carolina skyline.

"This is what I call a perfect beach day." The woman holding the brush spoke softly to herself as she surveyed the shore. Day trippers dotted the sand here and there; blankets and beach towels were spread out and anchored against the wind by coolers and discarded sandals. A small castle was under construction a few feet away. Squeals of delight saturated the air as three small children overturned buckets of moist sand, sculpting it into turrets. Their mother, in a broad-brimmed straw hat, hovered over them waving a bottle of sunscreen as they scrambled to avoid her grasp.

Adjusting the canvas stool beneath her, the artist caught sight of a young woman standing in the waves. Her small frame was dressed in white jean shorts and a yellow t-shirt and her chestnut hair was pulled high off her face in a ponytail. She appeared preoccupied, staring out to sea, motionless, one hand raised to shade her eyes from the sun. After a moment, she turned and slowly approached stopping just a few feet away.

Ava smiled and nodded hello. "I've seen you here before. I love your paintings. They're so beautiful." She paused, not sure what else to say.

"Thank you," the painter replied, bending down to retrieve another stool. She patted the green fabric top. "Have a seat. I always have room for company."

"Oh, I don't want to bother you." Ava was hesitant, but the woman insisted. She relaxed on the stool and watched the woman work.

The canvas was a swirl of blue and white voluminous clouds that magically appeared beneath the painter's brush strokes. Ava watched, fascinated as each new detail emerged. "How long does it take you to finish one?"

"Not long." The woman rested her brush on the pallet and turned to look at Ava. Wisps of her white hair blew gently around her face as she extended her hand. "My name is Beverly. Beverly Gilchrist."

Ava was immediately drawn to Beverly's easy warmth. "I'm Ava Dell," she said, feeling the corners of her mouth lift. "It's really nice to meet you."

"Are you on vacation, Ava?" Beverly picked up the brush again and continued to paint.

"Sort of. My family has a cottage down the beach." Reluctant to share too much, Ava was polite, but reserved. Instead she asked, "Do you live here, or are you just visiting?"

"I do now," Beverley answered. "I'm not from here originally, but it has always felt like home to me. My house is over towards Halsey Pier." She pointed in the opposite direction from Ava's cottage. "It's small, but it has everything I need. Is your family with you?"

Ava hedged. "No. How about you?"

"I used to come and visit my sister Helene. She and her husband had a place a few streets back from the beach. I loved everything about it, especially spending time with my two nephews. After I retired, I decided to get my own place. I was really lucky. A small cottage right on the shore came on the market, and I snatched it up before anyone else even realized it was for sale." Beverly smiled, clearly pleased with her good fortune.

"Do your sister and her family still live here?"

"Unfortunately, no. She and my brother-in-law moved to Charlotte to be closer to their two boys. Helene hated to leave, but she comes back once in a while and stays with me."

More squeals from the children building the sand castle pierced the air, competing with the sea gulls shrieking at the shore's edge. Ava breathed in the salt air and rubbed the glass of her necklace. "Do you live on your own?" As soon as the words were out, she felt self-conscious for prying into the personal life of someone she had just met. Sheepishly, she stared at her hands in her lap.

If Beverly noticed, she did not let on. "I do. It's just me. I used to work for an insurance company in Atlanta for years. I loved it there, there was always something to do. But once I retired, I wanted a slower pace. So I moved here and it was the best decision I've ever made. That's when I started painting and nothing makes me happier."

"You didn't paint before?"

"Nope." Beverly chuckled. "Evidently, I was a late bloomer."

"But you're so good," Ava complimented. "What made you start?"

"I used to walk along the beach every day, just like you." Beverly patted Ava's knee softly.

"There were always lots of people with easels doing their thing. One day, I noticed an older gentleman, Myles, creating the most beautiful seascape and I stopped to admire it. He told me painting was easy and offered to teach me the basics. Well, you didn't have to ask me twice! I ran into town and bought an easel, a few canvases, and some acrylics and voilà!"

"I would sit beside Myles while he taught me about color and different brushstrokes. But the best thing he ever showed me was how to capture a mood. It's like a snapshot in time; what do you want the viewer to take away? That 'take away' is the mood that you want to convey."

Ava nodded. "How do you decide what to paint? I know most people here do beach scenes but weren't you working on a house a few days ago?"

Beverly's eyes went wide with delight. "Yes! You're right. I was painting a house with gardens in the front yard and a large oak tree. It was a sweet little house, old and historic. You know that whole notion of 'if walls could talk?' I think if the walls in that house could talk they would reminisce about the many happy times that took place there. That's just the feeling it gave me."

"Who lives there? A friend of yours?" Ava asked.

"No. I don't know who lives there, but I wish I did." Beverly dipped her brush into a small cup of water and wiped it dry with a rag that hung from the easel.

Ava lifted her hand to block the sun from her eyes and squinted at Beverly. "Then why did you paint it?"

"Because," Beverly answered simply, "I had to."

CHAPTER 27

Ted was never far from Ava's thoughts. A few days into her self-exile, she allowed herself to remember how much they'd shared. Bits and pieces of their conversations ran through her mind. If she could turn back time, they would be sitting on the window seat at The Tea Cozy sharing oatmeal raisin cookies and sweet tea and arguing about the merits of going to a movie theater versus watching movies online. He was her friend, but really he was so much more than that. Ted was like the comfortable t-shirt that had been washed hundreds of times and was almost threadbare. It was the shirt you reached for the minute it came out of the dryer. She wondered how his parents and sister were coping with his death.

Her phone rang snapping her back to the present. Seeing that it was Casey, Ava felt obligated to answer it.

"Ava?" Casey sounded surprised. "You picked up!"

Sitting on the living room couch, Ava drew her legs underneath her, and answered quietly. "Hi Casey."

"Ava!" Casey repeated. "Where are you? Everyone's been asking me and I don't know what to tell them. Charlotte's on a rampage and Georgia and Kassi didn't even know there was a problem until I told them. Are you okay?"

Tears welled in Ava's eyes. Listening to Casey made her think of home. "I'm okay. I'm so sorry I left the way I did. I didn't know what else to do."

"Where are you Ava?" Casey asked, her voice heavy with worry.

Ava was reluctant to tell her but had no choice. It was not fair or right to keep Casey in the dark any longer.

"I'm at Sully Shores, but I don't want anyone to know." She rushed to explain. "I had to get away, Casey, and figure things out, but I know I was wrong to leave the way I did. I really messed up."

"Don't worry. I've got things under control. But people want to know where you are."

Ava winced. "Tell them I had unexpected business to take care of. If they keep asking, say that's all you know. Are you sure you're okay?"

"I'm fine," Casey assured her. "Remember, we said we'd get through this together."

"Okay, then. I'll call Georgia and Kassi and let them know where I am. As for Charlotte, thanks for covering for me."

"She was just in the other day. She's determined to find you and find out what happened."

Ava was not ready to face Charlotte. "Please don't tell anyone where I am," she pleaded.

"I won't," Casey agreed. "But you have to promise to pick up the phone when I call."

"I promise."

Casey hesitated. "One more thing. Are you planning to come back for Ted's funeral?"

Ava's stomach flip-flopped. She had not even allowed herself to think about that. "I'm not sure. When is it?"

"It hasn't been announced yet." Casey hated upsetting her. "They still have to do an autopsy to confirm the cause of death. I'll text you as soon as I know."

"Thanks. I'll be in touch." Before Casey could say any more, Ava disconnected the phone and tossed it on the sofa cushion. Wandering into her bedroom, she opened the dresser drawer and reached inside, cradling the red velvet box in her hands. She had not opened it since her arrival but talking to Casey had made her homesick. How were people back home dealing with Ted's death? Selfishly, she wondered if the pendulum could tell her how they felt about her.

Sitting on the edge of her bed, Ava brought the pendulum to her heart. "I'm putting it out to the universe. Please give me clarity to find the answers I'm looking for today," she prayed, holding her hand steady.

Repeating the question she had asked before leaving Wicks Falls, Ava whispered, "Did Ted take his own life?" She wanted to be sure it was the pendulum speaking and not her own emotions. Holding still for a brief moment, the pendulum slowly moved to the left. *Yes.*

Now it was time for the question she had dreaded asking most since the day she arrived. "Does everyone at home blame me for Ted's death?" She watched carefully for any sign of movement, but the pink crystal remained still. Disappointed, she understood there would be no clarity today; the pendulum was not going to answer her.

Ava put the pendulum away. Grabbing her sunglasses, she slipped on her flip-flops and headed to the beach. The physical act of walking felt good. Sweat from the sun glistened on her face, but she focused on each purposeful stride taking her closer to Beverly. She did not know why, but there was something about Beverly that just felt right.

The last few days, Ava had timed her walks for the early afternoon, knowing chances were good that Beverly would be on the beach, painting. It was the best light of the day, Beverly had shared with her, when the sun was over head and its rays were evenly distributed. But her favorite time of day was that hour before sunset when the light came over the water at its lowest angle and everything had a soft, golden glow to it. It was God's light she said, pure magic, but very difficult to capture on canvas because it was so fleeting.

Sure enough, Beverly was in her usual spot on the sand and Ava moved in her direction. Yesterday, she had been working on a seascape featuring a large pelican sitting on top of an old piling, the relic of a long gone mooring. The pelican's wings were stretched out majestically, suggesting it had just landed; its webbed feet gripped the worn wood. In the distance was Halsey Pier, dotted with fishermen casting rods over the side into the turquoise blue sea. So far, it was Ava's favorite. She loved the pelican's power and grace as it positioned its large body on such a small plane.

"Hi," she called to Beverly still a few feet away. Beverly peeked from around the canvas and waved, paintbrush in hand. Smiling at her new friend, Ava helped herself to the green canvas seat, the ocean at her back, the sun warm on her face. From her vantage, Ava could not see what Beverly was doing behind the easel, but guessed she was putting the finishing touches on the pelican picture.

"Ava!" Beverly exclaimed. "How are you? Isn't it a gorgeous day? There's a slight breeze every now and then that's delightful, and it keeps the paint from melting."

Shifting on the stool, Ava stretched her legs out, digging her heels into the white sand. "It's perfect. The beach is pretty quiet today."

Beverly took a moment to look around. "I love it. Not too busy, which for me means fewer distractions. How about you? How's your day going?"

"Okay, just trying to get things settled at the cottage. There's always so much to do when you haven't been here in a while."

Beverly understood. "That's why I try not to leave too often. I figure if it took me this long to find paradise, I'm going to squeeze every last minute out of the experience. Where's home for you when you're not at Sully Shores?" She asked.

"Not far from here." Ava was intentionally vague. "I've lived there almost two years and I have my own business; a small coffee shop. Before that, I was a business analyst in Laurelwood. That's where I grew up, but it was time for a change." Ava had not offered up much, but it was enough to make her feel better.

Beverly stopped painting for a moment and eyed Ava with interest. "What made you decided to open a coffee shop? That's a big leap from Corporate America."

"I've always loved to bake; it's a passion of mine," she explained. "Corporate America paid the bills, but I never really loved my job. When the opportunity for something new came along, I took it. Now I love what I do. Not everyone can say that."

"It's kind of like me with painting. Sometimes things need to fall into place for other things to happen. You're very lucky to do something that brings you so much joy. Does your family help out at the shop?"

"No. Both of my parents are gone; Dad died in a car accident a long time ago, and Mom had cancer. I don't have any brothers or sisters."

Beverly put her brush down. Kneeling next to Ava, she wrapped her in a heartfelt hug. "I'm so sorry."

Beverly's nurturing arms around her felt good. Melting into her embrace, Ava did not want to move. After a minute, she spoke.

"I practically grew up here," she said. "My parents and I came every summer." She touched her necklace.

Beverly noticed but said nothing as she held Ava's hand. "I firmly believe the sea has healing powers. If you're in pain, this is the place to be."

Ava gave her a quick smile. Beverly got it. "So," she said ready to change the subject, "What are you working on today? Is it the pelican? So far, he's my favorite."

Beverly stood upright, pulling Ava with her as she did. "Not today. Today there's a higher power in charge. Come look."

Retrieving her paintbrush, Beverly motioned for Ava to join her at the easel. "It's interesting, I'll give you that."

Standing next to Beverly, Ava struggled to hide her emotions as she looked at the painting. She bit her lip hard and stared at the image before her. Neutral beige tones framed the background. In the forefront, a red velvet box trimmed in silver, sat on a nondescript table. Draped over the box by a silver chain, its rose-colored sphere resting on the surface was Ava's pendulum.

CHAPTER 28

"What do you think?" Beverly took a step back, giving Ava a clear view of the painting.

She could not take her eyes off it. *How in the world?* Ava blinked rapidly as if closing her eyes would change what she saw; but the pendulum and the box remained on the canvas.

"Like you said," Ava spoke over her shoulder. "It's interesting."

The pendulum was exactly like hers, from the silver chain embedded with miniature stones to the quartz crystal dangling from its length. Charlotte had created it especially for her, empowering it with Ava's own strengths to guide and assist her whenever she needed. Pendulums were particular in their abilities, she remembered Charlotte saying, but not always original in design. Beverly could have seen a pendulum like Ava's somewhere else, but the box was definitely one-of-a-kind.

"It's a beautiful pendulum," she said, fishing for clues. "Where did you get it?"

"Oh! That's what it is? It's not mine. I've never seen it before." Beverly scratched her head, puzzled. She moved in for a closer look.

Keeping her expression carefully blank, Ava listened as Beverly talked.

"It's not unusual for me to paint things for people I know: family, friends, even casual acquaintances sometimes," she explained. "When it happens, this feeling takes over and I feel compelled to paint whatever I see in my head, like it's a message I'm supposed to pass on or something." She shrugged. "It sounds crazy, I know."

Ava was quiet, afraid to say anything that might give her away as Beverly continued to speak.

"Usually I can figure out who the paintings are for, but every now and then I'll paint something like this one." She pointed to her easel. "Not pendulums but other things that I can't explain or connect, but I don't dare get rid of them."

It was a good story, but Ava found it hard to believe. Anxious to get home, she said a quick good-bye to Beverly and jogged back to the cottage. Taking the front steps two at a time, she slammed the front door closed behind her and ran to the bedroom to check on the pendulum.

Relief washed over her as she lifted the red velvet box with silver trim from the dresser drawer. It was still there. Even knowing it was impossible for Beverly to have taken it, Ava had still wondered. And yet, how else could she explain the painting?

Somewhere in the house a floorboard creaked while an invisible breeze caused the bedroom window curtains to dance. Ava was spooked. No matter how hard she tried, she could not come up with a logical explanation. Wasting no time, she put the box back in the drawer and made a beeline for the porch.

The ocean view from Ava's chair was a soothing balm to her frayed nerves. Calm and distraction were what she needed right now, like that yoga class Ted had dragged her to last spring.

"Namaste," Ted whispered with one eye on her, his perfect tree pose reminding her of a strong oak, while she bent and wobbled like a weak sapling.

"Namaste, my ass," she had whispered back, making sure the instructor was out of earshot. "How is this contortion act supposed to be good for me again?"

Ted's sigh of exasperation nearly toppled her sapling. "Focus, Ava. Concentrate on what you're doing, and the rest will come. Oh, and don't forget to breathe; that's really important, too."

Shaking the memory clear, Ava pulled out her phone and pressed speed dial. Distraction came in many forms.

"Hi, Georgia. It's Ava."

"Ava! Where are you? How are you? I've been so worried." Hearing Georgia's voice, Ava's mood lightened instantly.

"I've been better, but I probably don't need to tell you that." The corner of her mouth lifted slightly picturing Georgia and Kassi. They knew her better than anyone.

"I wish you were here," Georgia said. "Are you at the cottage?"

"Yes. I'm spending a little quality time with me, myself and I right now."

"You mean you're hiding out."

Ava almost laughed. "I suppose you could call it that."

"Good. Stay there and don't hang up. I'm calling Kassi so we can have a three-way."

Moments later Kassi's voice sounded in Ava's ear. "Ava, my God we've been so worried about you. Why didn't you call?"

"I'm sorry, Kass." *It seems like that's all I've been saying lately.* Thinking of Ted, Ava could relate.

"I didn't mean to shut you out. I just needed some time on my own."

"If it weren't for Casey we wouldn't know anything," Kassi admonished before softening her tone. "We heard about Ted. I'm so sorry."

At the sound of his name, Ava burst into tears.

"Oh, Honey." Georgia comforted her friend like she would one of her kids. "It's okay. We're here for you. You know that, right?"

Ava nodded. "I do." She sniffed, using her sleeve as a tissue. "I don't know what I'd do without you guys."

"You never have to worry about that. We're not going anywhere."

An easy silence settled upon them as Kassi and Georgia waited for Ava to collect herself.

After a moment, she said, "Okay, I'm alright now. Can we just talk about something else for a minute? Georgia, how are the kids? Kassi, where does the job have you today?"

Georgia and Kassi took turns distracting Ava from her worries by catching her up on their own lives. Georgia's oldest was taking ballet lessons; her youngest had lost her first tooth.

"Can you believe the going rate for the Tooth Fairy is five dollars now?" she exclaimed, outraged.

"That's ridiculous. Give her a gold dollar coin instead," Kassi suggested. "It's worth more and it's shiny. Girls love shiny, no matter how old they are."

"I've noticed." Georgia's verbal jab was teasing.

"Speaking of which, what kind of bling did you buy yourself with your latest bonus?"

Kassi refused to apologize for her behavior. "Hey, I work hard. Very hard. There's nothing wrong with treating myself to a little something something every now and then."

"So what did you get?" Ava asked, tag teaming with Georgia.

"I have to admit, I outdid myself this time," Kassi confessed. "You'd love it Av, it's a pendant necklace, a beautiful rose quartz on a spectacular silver rope chain. It kind of reminds me of your pendulum, but different."

The words were out of her mouth before Kassi realized it.

"It's okay," Ava tried to ease Kassi's discomfort. "I know Casey told you guys what happened."

"Do you want to talk about it?" Kassi spoke quietly as if the question might upset Ava.

"I don't even know where to begin." Ava's voice was soft but steady, her mind racing with all the events that had brought her to this moment. "Ted is gone. I thought I could help him, I really did," she spoke with conviction. "But I screwed up."

"I don't believe that for a minute." Georgia was loyal through and through.

"It's true," Ava insisted. "I thought I knew what Ted was going through, why he was so stressed out. I thought it was just work."

"Well, it was, wasn't it?" Kassi tried to remember everything Casey had told her. "Embezzling funds from your job is a big deal."

"I know, but Ted would never do that."

"But Ava, they're saying he did." Kassi insisted, quietly.

"I honestly don't know what happened," Ava admitted. "That's the problem, I didn't realize how serious things were. God, I was so stupid; 'you can't do this alone, you need to ask for help.' That's what I told him. I was such an idiot."

"Ava, no," Georgia protested.

"It's true. If I'd been a better friend to Ted, I wouldn't have let him brush me off. I should have made him tell me what was really going on. But no, I thought I had it all figured out. Meanwhile, he was drowning. This is my fault."

"You're being too hard on yourself," said Georgia.

"Did you ever think maybe you're giving yourself too much credit?" Speaking her mind came naturally to Kassi. It wasn't in her nature to beat around the bush about anything, much less her best friend's misguided self-pity.

"Credit?" Ava couldn't believe it. "You think I'm taking credit for Ted's death?"

"For not stopping it." Kassi was calm, but resolute. "Honey, you didn't know what Ted was going through because he didn't want you to know, not because you're a bad friend. You're a great friend. Georgia, and I will attest to that.

And I'm sure you gave him good advice, too. I just think maybe Ted was beyond anyone's help."

Kassi's words fell on deaf ears as Ava thought about Ted and the note. *Maybe if I'd listened to you sooner.* She wished he had not listened to her at all. She wished he had trusted her enough to tell her everything.

Why didn't you tell me the truth? She wanted to know so badly it made her angry.

The conversation had reached an emotional impasse, and Ava didn't want to talk about it anymore.

"Let's change the subject, okay?"

CHAPTER 29

In the early dawn, the sky was a brilliant display of color that promised yet another beautiful day ahead. From her breakfast nook, Beverly watched the colorful theatrics, itching to capture the moving light show on canvas, but rooted to her chair.

She should have been on the beach; her easel and paint box were already at the door waiting for her, but Beverly didn't move. She was waiting too, with pencil in hand. This was how it always started when she painted for someone else. It was as if a firm hand rested on her shoulder, forcing her to be still until an image appeared clearly in her mind. As soon as it did, the hand lifted and she moved quickly, drawing the picture with broad swift strokes of a pencil before it could be erased from her memory.

The first time it had happened, she'd thought she was having a stroke. She had been washing up in her bathroom, preparing for bed. Suddenly, she could not speak, and her limbs were so heavy they felt numb. She had been paralyzed with fear. *What was happening?* Filling her lungs with deep concentrated breaths, she'd managed to grow calm, and the heaviness that had overwhelmed her, lifted.

In Beverly's newly clairvoyant state, everything was crystal clear and sharp, like her reflection in the bathroom mirror. Beneath her fingertips, familiar high cheekbones accentuated the smooth finish of her peaches-and-cream complexion; her blue eyes were brilliant like sapphires. But the longer she stared at herself, the more things began to change. A steely sheen replaced her peachy glow, and black circles darkened her eyes beyond recognition. She saw but could not feel the water that began to flow from her mouth like a faucet, steady and strong; the force of it seemed to morph her features into a series of changing and unfamiliar faces.

Just as suddenly as the mirage started, it stopped like a light switched on and off, and Beverly once again faced her own reflection. That first vision had shaken her to the core; the steel face haunting her day and night as she tried to read a book, cook a meal, or watch television. It was all she could see, until one day out of frustration, she had picked up her brush; maybe she could paint it out of her system and be rid of it for good.

Painting had been new to her then, as she had honed her skills under Myles tutelage; the senior artist seemed to think she had a natural talent for capturing the sentiment of Mother Nature's domain. But the steel mask Beverly saw in the mirror was unlike anything she had ever painted before.

It took more than a week for her to replicate it in acrylic, but she was driven by an unexplained sense of urgency that vanished as soon as the work was complete. The weird disturbance that had consumed her life for days on end was gone leaving her confused and annoyed.

Standing in front of her creation, she wondered what was the point? And more importantly, what was she supposed to do with it now? It wasn't exactly her taste, but she had put too much into it to just throw it away.

"Hello! Aunt Beverly?" Her nephew Logan called through the front screen door. "Mom sent me to pick you up for dinner. I'm your designated driver so you two can drink your Chardonnay."

Beverly opened the door and welcomed Logan inside. "Your mom's a smart woman," she chuckled, giving him a quick hug. "Thank you for doing this. Wine is exactly what I need right now."

While Beverly grabbed a sweater from her bedroom, Logan moved to examine her latest art project.

"This is so cool Aunt Bev, but how did you know?"

"How did I know what?" Beverly stood beside him. "This darn thing wouldn't leave me alone until I painted it. I don't even know what it is."

Logan was surprised. "You're kidding."

"Nope." Seeing it through her nephew's eyes, Beverly was proud. "Not bad for something I dreamed up."

Logan looked doubtful. "I'm not so sure about that. This looks exactly like METALmorphosis."

"Metal what?"

"METALmorphosis. It's a sculpture in Charlotte," Logan explained. "Actually, it's a kinetic sculpture of a human head. It's powered by water that moves all the pieces into different faces so that it's constantly changing."

Beverly was stunned. "You mean this, this thing? It's real?"

"Uh huh, very real. It's part of this huge corporate park in Charlotte. It's pretty famous, I guess. I just learned about it myself. I interviewed for a job there."

Logan pulled out his phone and googled METALmorphosis. "See," he said, showing her a picture of the sculpture. "That's it."

Beverly stared at the picture of a three-dimensional face made of polished steel. Like her painting, water spouted from its oversized mouth, and poured into a surrounding reflecting pool. She squinted, barely able to discern the forty shape-shifting layers of metal that formed the kinetic sculpture. Except for the 3D, she had captured it perfectly.

"I swear I've never seen this before," she said, handing

the phone back to Logan. "Wait. I thought you were offered a position in New York. Your mom called in tears because her baby's moving so far away."

"I was." He tucked his phone into his pocket, smiling at his aunt. "And then I got the call from Charlotte."

"I've been working with this amazing recruiter," he elaborated. "New York is a fantastic opportunity, but then Charlotte came along, and he thought I should hear them out before committing to anything."

"So, what happened?" A small frown creased Beverly's forehead.

"I met with the people in Charlotte a week or so ago, and yesterday they extended an offer. It's a really awesome opportunity, but I'm just not sure; New York is solid too, and I did speak with them first if that counts for anything."

Beverly sympathized. "Sounds like a tough decision, but not a bad position to be in."

"I know, you're right." The twenty-six-year-old beside her sounded so young. "But I kind of wish someone would just tell me what I should do."

Lost in thought, they gazed at the canvas in companionable silence.

"I paint landscapes," Beverly said.

"What?"

"I paint landscapes: clouds in the sky, water, that kind of thing." She pointed at METALmorphosis. "This came to me out of nowhere. I've never seen it before and I certainly didn't imagine it. So why would I suddenly do something like this? There's no logical explanation I can think of except maybe it has a purpose. Maybe it's a message. . . .for you."

Logan stifled a laugh. "I'm sorry, Aunt Bev, that just sounds a little out there to me."

Equally perplexed, Beverly agreed. "I know, it's strange, but how else do you explain it?"

"Let's say you're right. What's the message here?"

Logan humored his favorite aunt. She loved him and his brother, Nathan, like a mother, and spoiled them like an aunt with her zany fun and high-spirited antics. He had always assumed that was why his dad often said, "there's a little bit of crazy in you, Beverly." But maybe this is what he meant.

"Don't look at me like that," Beverly scolded. "This is new to me too, you know, but I don't think it's coincidental, my strange painting and your current dilemma. You're trying to choose between two jobs, right?"

Logan nodded, and Beverly continued, thinking out loud.

"If you were supposed to go to New York, it could have been the Empire State Building or the Freedom Tower. But METALmorphosis is in Charlotte, and I didn't even know you were interviewing there. If I had to guess, I'd say this is telling you to take the job in Charlotte."

Logan was still on the fence but warming to Beverly's theory.

"A minute ago, you were wishing someone would tell you what to do. I think that's exactly what's happening here. You should go to Charlotte."

Back in the breakfast nook, the pencil in Beverly's hand began to move across the sketchpad on the table in front of her, interrupting her memories. Logan was the first to benefit from her revelations, but others had followed. Over time, she had even grown accustomed to the episodes, recognizing the symptoms and what was to follow. Each time was exciting to Beverly as she waited for an image to appear in her mind, like searching for the prize in a box of Cracker Jacks. Always atypical from her usual artistic form, Beverly had come to view her creations as a special kind of communication, one that used art to translate meaning.

Beneath the pencil's point, shapes were taking form: the columned fascia of a stately building, a great clock embedded beneath its apex. Beverly frowned. It was another mystery, just like the pendulum. She would paint it anyway; just like METALmorphosis and all the others, it would haunt her until she did.

CHAPTER 30

From her perch, curled up on the faded blue couch, Ava watched the raindrops splatter across the windows as tears wetted her cheeks. Thunderous clouds threatened outside, dark and stormy, making both the ocean and her stomach churn as she pictured what was happening right now in Wicks Falls.

Casey had called days earlier to let her know. "The funeral is Wednesday, Ava. Ten o'clock at St. Michael's. You'll be there, right?"

She had not said 'yes' or 'no,' promising only to do her best. But she knew her best would never get her through it --

not the moving service or tearful eulogies, not the heart-wrenching sight of Ted's casket or his heartbroken family, and most especially not all the questions she knew people were dying to ask her. *Did Ted tell you anything? Was he acting differently? Did you have any idea?*

Instead, from the safety of her couch, Ava imagined what she was missing. She could see the sleek black hearse idling outside of St. Michael's Church, waiting for the exodus of mourners to emerge. The crowd is a sea of black umbrellas offering weak shelter against the driving rain as the people scramble to their cars. The hearse moves slowly, pulling away from the curb, a procession of cars trailing behind it as it winds through the center of town at a snail's pace. She pictures it passing the park and the movie theater, past The Tea Cozy and the post office, to the Cemetery of Immaculate Souls where Ted will be laid to rest in the family plot. Squeezing her eyes tight, she tried unsuccessfully to clear the image from her mind and started to sob.

At her home on Halsey Pier, Beverly painted in her studio, feeling solemn and sad. Something more than the weather was dampening her mood, but she couldn't put her finger on it. Stepping back from her work, she crossed her arms, holding the brush to her lips like a long cigarette holder, and studied the canvas. Wet and gloomy and slightly ominous, the image matched the weather perfectly.

The columned architecture and gray majesty of the noble building before her suggested an historic origin. Civil War-era, maybe? She squinted leaning close to examine the ornate clock face that prominently graced the façade's peak, for non-existent clues, but to no avail. She sighed heavily, disappointed.

This was the occasional curse of her gift: not knowing, immediately or ever, who were the intended recipients of her special paintings, but she considered it a gift all the same and felt blessed to have it. For Beverly, there was no better feeling than helping her loved ones and friends sort through some of life's dilemmas and challenges, and since her closest relationships were also the most familiar to her, it was seldom hard to identify the beneficiary of her work. She ran a quick mental check of all her nearest and dearest, trying to link the painting to one of them in a meaningful way, but came up empty. She sighed again, removing the brush from her mouth and returned to her post in front of the easel. Beverly resumed painting. Maybe when it was finished, it would come to her.

After two days of bone-soaking dreariness, the sun finally emerged, and Ava couldn't wait to get outside. The weather-imposed solitary confinement had taken its toll on her. She slipped on a sweatshirt pulling the zipper up to her chin and walked towards the beach.

Pent up energy carried her down the sand towards Halsey Pier and Beverly, her only friend here. Meeting on the beach each day, they had logged more hours than Ava could count talking, laughing, and getting to know each other better.

Spotting her now, Ava began to jog the short stretch over to Beverly. Per usual, she was at her easel, focused and blind to Ava's arrival.

"Hey!" Ava gasped, fighting to catch her breath, her

hands on her thighs for support. "Wow. I have got to start working out!"

Handing her a bottle of water, a dubious Beverly watched as Ava chugged it down. "I thought you didn't believe in exercise."

"I didn't. I mean, I don't, but look at me. I'm huffing and puffing like the Big Bad Wolf. I'm too young for that."

"True," Beverly agreed. "But I don't think zero to sixty in thirty seconds is the way to do it either." Returning the empty water bottle to her small cooler, she gave Ava a fresh one. "Drink it slowly or you'll get hiccups," she cautioned.

"Okay, Mom," Ava teased, but she followed Beverly's instructions. Plopping onto the beach stool already set-up for her, she burrowed her feet into the cool, damp sand.

"Thank God the rain finally stopped. I was going stir-crazy. How about you?" She glanced at Beverly working.

"Mmm hmm. A little bit." Beverly cocked her head to one side, considering her next strokes. "But I sort of didn't mind either. It was perfect for what I'm working on now."

"Is it a new one?"

Beverly nodded. "It came to me a couple of mornings ago."

On her stool, Ava tensed afraid to ask. "You mean it's one of your special paintings?"

"Yes." Beverly nodded again. "It's nearly finished, and quite lovely, but there's something kind of menacing about it, too. See for yourself."

Ava's feet rooted deep into the sand, willing her to stay put, but she couldn't. Rising from the stool, she forced herself to go stand beside Beverly, who waited for Ava's reaction. She inhaled sharply, bringing her hand to her open mouth and stared hard at the Wicks Falls post office. Beverly had captured it perfectly: the entrance doors that opened and closed like a giant's mouth protected from the elements beneath the covered portico, the pockmarks of historic bullet holes scattered across the exterior walls, and the elegant signature clock.

"Do you recognize it?" Beverly's voice was soft and low, a whisper in Ava's ear as she stood lost in the image.

Ava didn't answer her.

Beverly laid a concerned hand on Ava's shoulder. "Maybe you should sit down." Guiding Ava to the nearby stool, she grabbed the bottle of water from the sand where Ava had left it and handed it to her.

"Drink some water," she urged. "You look like you've just seen a ghost."

Ava grimaced. Even here at Sully Shores, she was haunted.

"Oh Beverly, you have no idea."

CHAPTER 31

The next day, Ava picked her way carefully over the large jutting rocks of the jetty where even on this beautiful day, waves crashed against it, making the granite arm slippery and treacherous. Trading beachcombing for rock climbing, she would have done anything to avoid Beverly right now.

Through sheer luck, she had somehow managed to escape Beverly's inquisition about the post office painting, but she was not taking any chances. The only way to elude Beverly's questions was to avoid her altogether. Not forever, just until Ava was ready to tell Beverly her truth.

Reaching the end of the jetty, she stood facing the horizon, the ocean breeze blowing her unbound hair away from her face. She was certain the paintings were signs intended for her, but what did they mean?

Let your heart be your compass. She heard her mother

encouraging her forward and knew what it meant: she had to be honest with herself and follow her heart; she had to talk to Beverly. She had created the incriminatory paintings; it only made sense that she would be the one to help Ava understand them. It was a leap of faith trusting her new friend with the knowledge of what she had done, but it was a risk Ava had to take. She pulled out her phone and called Beverly.

"Ava! I'm so glad you called. I need to see you. Can you come over?" Excitement crept into Beverly's voice. "I've got something I want to show you."

Ava half-jogged, half-walked the short trip over to Beverly's cottage, alternately eager and hesitant to see her. Before she could knock, the front door swung open and Beverly pulled her inside.

"I'm so glad you're here."

Without further ado, she grasped Ava's hand, leading her down a short hallway, past the tidy kitchen and breakfast nook, past a cozy sitting room dressed in warm desert tones and Aztec prints that reminded Ava of Beverly herself.

"They're all here in my studio," she said, letting Ava enter first. Just inside, Ava paused, soaking in the brilliant light that streamed through the open windows, illuminating the predominantly glass space. Three easels stood to one side, lined up like soldiers waiting for inspection. To her right, an oversized hutch of golden oak with drawers and cupboards that housed Beverly's art supplies rested against the room's only solid wall.

"So, this is where the magic happens." She smiled, reverently. "Kind of like Santa's Workshop."

Beverly laughed. "It is often full of surprises," she agreed. "This is where all of my special paintings come to me. I prefer to be outside for my landscapes."

"That makes sense." Ava walked to the center of the room, turning a slow 360 degrees until Beverly stood in front of her holding a glass of wine in each hand. She offered one to Ava.

"I keep a wine fridge over there." She tipped her chin towards the hutch. "For when I need a little extra inspiration." She touched her glass to Ava's. "Or, liquid courage."

Ava frowned. "What do you mean?"

"I want to show you something," she said, "but first I have to tell you, I've been working like a maniac these past few days. One painting after another in a very short period of time." Beverly was practically breathless.

"That's unusual?"

"For me it is. I don't think I've ever finished three pictures like these three in such quick succession before."

Gently, she gripped Ava's elbow and guided her to the other side of the room where the three easels stood. Each was shrouded in cloth, mysteries waiting to be revealed. Without a word, Beverly removed the first sheet.

Ava tensed seeing the pendulum. It used to make her

feel special, powerful; now she only felt ashamed. She looked at Beverly who observed her quietly before moving on to the next easel.

Beverly removed the second sheet, stepping aside to give Ava a full view of the Wicks Falls post office. A new element had been added. Two people sat on the sidewalk bench at the bottom of the steps: a man and a woman, fair haired and dark. Ava bit her lip, hard.

"You haven't seen this one before," Beverly remarked, before taking the third and final sheet away. "What do you think?"

It was a painting of Ted, her Ted, sitting in the window booth at The Tea Cozy. He was dressed in his business casual uniform, khakis and a button-down shirt. On his right hand, he wore Grandpa Clyde's ring.

Ava looked at Beverly through tear-filled eyes. "I don't understand. How did you know?"

Beverly was sympathetic. "I'm so sorry, Ava. I wasn't entirely sure that these were meant for you, but I started to suspect after I showed you this one that day on the beach." She pointed to the second painting. "You were so upset."

"I don't know this young man," she continued, speaking about Ted, "but the timing of it was such that I figured it had to be connected to the other two, that they were all part of the same story."

"They're all part of *my* story." Ava could not keep from blurting it out.

Maybe it was the wine; Ava's glass was empty although she did not recall drinking from it. Squaring her shoulders, she lifted her head high with confidence certain that the time had finally come. She was ready to talk; about her and Ted, about the pendulum, all of it.

CHAPTER 32

"Will you come over to my place?" Ava needed to show Beverly her story, not just tell her. "I want you to see something."

"Right now?" Beverly asked, surprised by the invitation.

"If that's okay?" Ava hoped she was not asking too much.

Beverly did not hesitate. "Absolutely. I'll drive. Let me just grab my purse. It's in the kitchen."

While she waited, Ava wondered briefly if she was making a mistake confiding in Beverly, but she pushed those thoughts away. She needed to talk.

Beverly returned with her purse slung across her body, waving car keys. "Okay, I'm ready to go. Let's just bring these along." She walked over to the easels, removing the three paintings from their ledges.

"I'll get those for you." Ava reached for the canvases, holding the vignettes of her life in her arms.

When they pulled into Ava's driveway, Beverly cooed her approval. "Oh, this is beautiful," she said taking in the cottage and the surrounding rose bushes. "I can see why you love it here. It's much quieter than where I am near the pier." The only noise came from a seagull squawking overhead. "It really is paradise, isn't it?"

Ava brought them around the house to the beachfront. Waving her arm at the horizon, she smiled. "This is my slice of heaven. When my parents bought this place years ago, it was just a little shack. It still is really, but they worked hard to make it as special as they could."

They went inside, and Ava gestured for Beverly to have a seat on the sofa. "Please, make yourself comfortable. I'll get us some more wine."

Returning with two glasses of Chardonnay, Ava handed one to Beverly before sitting in a side chair. She noticed that Beverly had lined up the pictures against the wall: first the pendulum, then the post office and finally, Ted. She stared briefly at the picture of Ted, and wished yet again that he were there, too.

"I'm not sure where to start. It feels like my life has been unraveling in slow motion." Ava curled her legs beneath her. "I guess maybe Wicks Falls."

"Where's that?" Beverly interjected as she settled in on the sofa.

Ava smiled. "That's where The Tea Cozy is."

"Okay." Beverly nodded her head.

"Actually, let me start before Wicks Falls. I told you my dad passed when I was young." Ava touched the sea glass necklace before continuing. "Then my mom got cancer. When she died, I remember thinking I must have a huge black cloud hanging over my head."

"I'm so sorry." Beverly touched Ava's arm, offering her condolences.

"My mother was a spiritual person. I don't necessarily mean religious, although she very much believed in God. She was convinced that some people were especially sensitive to things that others couldn't see. You know, intuition, sixth sense, that sort of thing. Of course, that meant she was also convinced of an afterlife; because the signs and messages had to come from somewhere, right? To her, this sixth sense was a responsibility, but more importantly she viewed it as a gift."

"A gift." Beverly repeated thoughtfully.

"Yes. She was convinced that I had the same abilities she did. You know, when I was younger sometimes I just felt I knew things. There was this energy around me poking and prodding to get my attention, but I usually ignored it." Ava paused and chuckled softly. "Don't worry, I didn't see dead people or anything like that. Anyway, fast forward to college. I met a woman who told me that I knew things that others didn't. She said it was a gift and that it was my choice whether or not I wanted to accept it."

"This woman called it a gift, too?" Beverly asked. "A little more than coincidence, don't you think?"

"It certainly got me thinking," Ava admitted. "I was young though. I'm not sure I wanted to take the time to figure it all out. My mother begged me just to keep an open mind, which brings us to Wicks Falls."

Ava shifted in the chair, moving her legs to keep them from falling asleep. "After my mother died, I desperately needed a fresh start. I decided to open my coffee shop somewhere new, where there wouldn't be any painful memories. My real estate agent was a woman named Charlotte Boyer. We had barely met when she started talking to me about my energy. I remember thinking 'Here we go again.' But I was older, and maybe, finally ready to think about it. We had a conversation about intuition and signs and messages and how some people are more receptive to them than others. Turns out, Charlotte knew a lot about these things."

"The more we talked, the more I think she was convinced that she could be a mentor to me. After we found The Tea Cozy property, she gave me the pendulum. I had no idea what it was, but it was beautiful, and she told me that it could make my life full."

Beverly's eyes widened, as she pointed to the first picture

in her line-up. "Like the one I painted?"

"Exactly like the one you painted," Ava replied. "I wasn't sure at first whether it was something I would use. It seemed a little 'hocus pocus' to me. But with practice, I began to see that the pendulum really did seem to work. I'm not sure if you're familiar with them, but they're used for affirmation. You ask the pendulum 'yes' or 'no' questions and it answers either way. Charlotte also used a pendulum. She told me over and over that I was just a messenger; that it should never be about me. I wish I had listened."

"What do you mean?" Beverly waited patiently as Ava paused to take a sip of wine. Liquid courage Beverly had called it.

"Turns out Wicks Falls was the perfect place for me. It's small and friendly with really caring people. It's charming with a park and a town green and a main street lined with beautiful buildings. When I was first researching the town with Charlotte, I told her my favorite building by far, was the post office."

Beverly pointed to the next painting. "I'm guessing that's the post office?"

"It is," Ava confirmed before continuing. "The Tea Cozy became my baby and the more successful it became, the more I knew I was where I was meant to be. I was learning the business at the same time I was learning how to use the pendulum. Somewhere along the way, the two things merged. I became more spiritual, like my mom, more mindful of how things might be connected. Her mantra was that everything happened for a reason and I began to understand that the more closely we pay attention to the signs, the better we can navigate our way through life." Ava paused. "Does that sound a little hokie?"

"Not at all." Beverly shook her head. "There's a reason for the expression 'with age comes wisdom,' although that would make me much wiser than you. But I definitely believe that the older we get, the more we appreciate that life truly is a journey."

Ava nodded, agreeing. "As I became more in tune with everything, I started to infuse that spirituality into The Tea Cozy. I used colors that were meaningful; I decorated with crystals for good energy, lit incense and essential oils to create a mood, all that stuff. My customers noticed and started asking me about these things. One thing led to another, and I started consulting the pendulum for friends and regulars. That led to Wicked Wednesdays."

"Wicked Wednesdays?" Beverly asked. "It sounds like a Broadway show."

"It does, doesn't it?" Ava agreed. "Wicked Wednesdays happen twice a month at night when The Tea Cozy is closed. I consult the pendulum for anyone interested, and another gal reads tarot cards. It's a social thing, but I really did feel like I was doing good by these people, that I was helping them somehow. Charlotte didn't see it that way."

"Why? Wasn't Charlotte happy that you'd finally learned to use your gifts, especially since you were using the pendulum she gave you to help people?" Beverly's confusion was understandable.

"Not really. Charlotte was firm from the beginning that the pendulum was a serious matter. She thought Wicked Wednesdays was a bit of a dog and pony show; that it was more about the wine and cheese we served than the spirituality. I didn't think so, but her disapproval was clear. She reminded me repeatedly, that my job was to act as a medium between the questions asked and the answers given. Even so, I thought my intuition and insight were better than most. I felt it was my duty to tell them what I knew."

"I can understand that. You thought you were being helpful. And I'm guessing people responded positively to you."

"I did feel like I was making a difference. But that's the problem. It became more about me and less about the pendulum." Ava took another sip of wine and stared at Beverly's paintings. "Which brings me to Ted."

Once more, Beverly pointed to her paintings, the third and final one. "That must be Ted."

"That's Ted." Tears rushed to Ava's eyes, but she quickly blinked them back. Too many tears had been shed for her actions since she had arrived at Sully Shores and they needed to stop.

"Is Ted your husband?" Beverly asked seeing Ava's tears.

"Oh my God, no!" Ava said, almost too loudly. "Ted was gay. But he was one of my best friends. At first, he was a regular customer, and then we became close. 'Besties' we'd say. He really was my better half."

"Ted never believed in the pendulum or signs or any of the things that had become important to me. We had more than a few arguments about it until we just agreed to disagree. Anyway, several weeks before I came here, Ted started acting differently. He was distracted and moody all the time, and he kept apologizing for silly things. He just wasn't himself. I didn't know what was going on and he wouldn't tell me. Then, all of a sudden, it got really bad. I offered to consult the pendulum for him. He told me not to bother, but I insisted. I was convinced that he was working too much to please his boss."

"If he had told you what was wrong, I'm sure you would have helped him make sense of things. Did you ever find out what was upsetting him? Did he fix it himself?" Beverly asked.

Ava exhaled loudly, releasing her darkest secret. "Not exactly. Ted's dead, Beverly. He took his own life, and it's my fault. I told him I had consulted the pendulum, but then I told him what I thought he should do. I insisted he talk to his boss and everything would work out. He died that day."

Ava glanced furtively at Beverly. "I crossed the line in so many ways; I just had to get out of Wicks Falls. I knew eventually Charlotte would figure out what I had done. The thought of her judging me, of everyone blaming me was just too much."

Beverly's voice was full of emotion as she placed her hand over her heart. "Ava, I am so, so sorry to hear about Ted. I had a strange feeling when I was painting that picture, almost as though there was a heaviness weighing down on me. But why would he take his own life? I don't understand."

Uncurling her legs, Ava pushed herself out of the chair. "I want to show you something. I'll be right back." She hurried to the bedroom and out of Beverly's sight.

Beverly sank back against the sofa cushions, remembering how she had felt while painting the three pictures. She recalled a sense of urgency and something else, too, like gravity pressing on her shoulders and creating a weight that she now understood.

Ava returned and took a seat next to Beverly. Placing all but one of the items she'd retrieved from the bedroom on the coffee table in front them, she lifted the red velvet box with silver trim from her lap and carefully opened the lid.

"This is my pendulum," she said, showing Beverly the pink quartz crystal on a silver chain identical to the one she had painted.

Holding out her hand, Beverly took the pendulum and studied it closely. "This is it! This is exactly what I saw, what I painted. I distinctly remember all of these colorful stones in the chain. It's beautiful."

Ava picked a note card up from the table and handed it to Beverly. "This came in the mail a few days after Ted's body was discovered."

The script was neat and orderly and Beverly's heart broke reading it.

Ava,

I didn't get to Charlie in time, but I wanted you to know that at least I tried. I should never have doubted you and your pendulum. Maybe if I'd listened to you sooner this wouldn't have happened. I'm sending you my grandfather's ring for safekeeping. You're more worthy of it than I'll ever be. I am so sorry.

Ted

"His grandfather's ring?"

Ava placed the hematite jewelry in Beverly's hand.

"I saw this so clearly when I was painting. Such a small detail, I couldn't for the life of me understand why it felt so important to include it. But now it makes sense. But, Ava, why do you feel responsible for Ted's death?"

"He says it right there, in his note that he never should have doubted me and the pendulum. But he didn't know the whole story. It wasn't the pendulum, it was me; I told him what I thought he needed to do. I pushed him to it."

Beverly hugged Ava. "Oh Honey, this isn't your fault. You can't make someone take his own life. Ted was fighting his own demons and obviously his judgment was clouded. You can't blame yourself. Is that why you're here? Are you afraid that everyone blames you?"

Ava hated to admit it. "Yes. I'm such a hypocrite. Ted and I had a fight one time about the tools people use to support their beliefs and how you shouldn't judge what works for someone else. But that's exactly what I did. I told people what a powerful tool the pendulum was, but when it wouldn't answer me, I answered for it. I think I just wanted Ted to need me."

She continued. "Ted didn't even want my advice, but I gave it to him anyway. I was so sure I knew all the answers. When people back home find out, they'll think I'm a complete fraud. How could I have gotten it so wrong that my best friend ended his life?"

Beverly gently returned the items to Ava before she spoke. "You're being way too hard on yourself. We all make our own decisions in life. I hope you don't take this the wrong way, but even if you provide some insight or advice to those that seek you out, they're still accountable for what they do. Your gifts don't have the power to make people do anything they don't want to do, Ava. Something was dreadfully wrong in Ted's life and regardless of what you might have said to him, he made his own decision. It's like me with my paintings. I don't always know who the messages are for, but I have an obligation to create and deliver them. And that's the end of it. What happens after that is beyond my control. Go home, Ava. Hiding out here is not the answer."

"But, I'm afraid I've ruined everything."

Beverly's smile was warm. "You're human. You're not perfect, none of us are. I bet it's never even occurred to your friends that it was anyone's decision other than Ted's to do what he did. What they probably don't understand is why you disappeared. You might be surprised to find that you've judged yourself much more harshly than anyone else."

Beverly straightened her linen pants as she stood. "You know sometimes, when you think things are falling apart, it might just be that they're falling into place." She collected her handbag, and readied to leave. "I'm going home now. Keep the paintings, they were meant for you anyway."

Ava followed her to the door with a sense of hope. Beverly was the right person to have purged her heart to. A slight sense of guilt still lingered within her, but thanks to Beverly's wisdom, she was ready to move forward and leave it behind. "Thank you for listening. What would I do without you?"

Beverly smiled and walked to her car, giving a wave as she slipped into the front seat.

Standing at the screen door watching Beverly drive away, Ava knew she was right. It was time for her to go home, too. No more running away, no more hiding.

A gust of warm air tickled her ear.

Everything happens for a reason.

CHAPTER 33

The car looked like an overstuffed mushroom, but instead of crabmeat, it was bursting with suitcases and trash bags full of incidentals. Once she had made her mind up to go home, Ava had gotten down to business: packing and organizing the things she wanted to bring back to Wicks Falls and cleaning the cottage. Her time with Beverly, sharing the weight of her secrets and fears had been more than therapeutic, it was an enormous release, like she had been holding her breath and finally let it go. If Beverly was right, and God, Ava hoped she was, then she should not be afraid to go back.

She scanned her bedroom, searching for more to pack

and spotted the red velvet box on her dresser. It called to her. Drawing the pendulum from the box, she carried it to the living room, and made herself comfortable on the couch. She had a good feeling that today the pendulum would finally tell her the truth.

Raising the pendulum to eye level, she spoke confidently. "I'm putting it out to the universe. Please help me get clarity today to the questions I have. Know that I approach you with sincerity in my heart and openness in my mind."

Releasing a deep breath Ava calmly asked, "Did Ted take his own life?" Consistent with its previous message, the pendulum swayed to the left. *Yes.*

"Did I cause Ted's death?" She stared at the pink quartz, willing herself to be patient. Within seconds, the pendulum swung to the right. *No.*

She felt better, but still had doubts. She asked the pendulum again, this time posing her question differently. "Could I have done anything to prevent Ted's death?" Again, she cautioned herself to wait. It was not necessary; the pendulum moved swiftly to the right. *No.*

Thank you, God. The last piece of guilt she had been carrying inside her melted away. It was time to move on even though life without Ted was impossible to imagine. She could never turn back the clock, but maybe one day she would understand why such horrible things had happened to such a good man.

The late afternoon sun was starting to inch to the west as Ava stepped onto the beach. She was going back to Wicks

Falls tomorrow. Casey already knew to expect her, and Kassi and Georgia had both promised to stop by in the coming weeks. It was time to put her life back on track, but first, she wanted to find Beverly.

The beach had a few stragglers this time of day, most of the tourists had returned to their hotels and the fishermen and beach painters were long gone. As she made her way towards Halsey Pier, Ava thought about Beverly. She was a special woman and a true friend; Ava was lucky to know her. She thought about Charlotte, too, and the differences between the two women. One took guidance from her gift the other gave it. She admired Beverly's generous spirit, making sure her special paintings and their messages got to their rightful owners. It was inspiring, the way she balanced her spiritual side with everyday living; Ava hoped she could do the same with the pendulum.

As she approached the pier, Ava spotted Beverly sitting in a beach chair, low to the sand. She held the brim of her large floppy hat, fighting the breeze that threatened to take it away. Ava followed her gaze to the sea, where two pelicans perched upon an old piling, jutting out of the water. It reminded her of her favorite picture.

"Hey you," Ava called, trying not to startle her. "Where are your easel and paints?"

She took a seat in the sand next to Beverly. "I thought you'd be out here working on a nice, serene seascape after all of those paintings you did for me."

Beverly's smile was warm and genuine. "Not today. Today I wanted to concentrate on you. How are you doing?

Have you given any thought to what we talked about yesterday?"

Ava nodded. "Definitely. You were right. I just couldn't believe Ted would take his own life; it was easier to blame myself. I guess it doesn't make much sense now. I thought it was just one more thing to add to that big black cloud that's been hanging over me since I was kid." Ava sighed.

"I'm glad you understand that. Even with your gifts, people have to make their own decisions." Beverly shifted, so she was facing Ava.

"My mother used to say the same thing, 'Your life, your decisions, Ava.' These last couple of weeks, I've certainly taken a very long and honest look at myself. I saw a lot of things I didn't like."

"Oh, Ava." Beverly reached for her hand, holding it tightly. "It bears repeating: don't be so hard on yourself. You're a wonderful, caring person. We all should take stock of our lives periodically, I know I do."

Ava was silent, staring at the sea. Finally, she turned to Beverly. "I'm going back to Wicks Falls tomorrow."

"I'm glad to hear that," Beverly said quietly. "I'll miss you, but that's where your life is. And don't worry; Charlotte will come around."

"I've thought a lot about Charlotte, too. I'm sure she's disappointed in me, but I'll have to wait and see. No sense worrying before then."

"She may just need your reassurance that you appreciate

and respect what she's taught you." Beverly paused. "I'll miss you, Ava. You've been such a bright spot in my life."

"Me too." She squeezed Beverly's hand. "I realized something else after you left yesterday. I've been avoiding Sully Shores because it was too painful, too many memories. But now I know that as much as I miss my parents I'm happy here not sad."

"And another thing -- I'm coming back here as often as I can. It's not that far from Wicks Falls, and Casey and I have both learned the hard way that she can manage The Tea Cozy while I'm gone. I'll call you when I'm back in town."

Beverly laughed. "I wouldn't have it any other way. It sounds like you've found a way to have the best of both worlds."

Ava stood and brushed the powdery sand off her shorts. "I think so. Mom always told me to look for life's blessings. Turns out I didn't have to look very far at all. Ted's gone, and I can't bring him back, but I still have so many wonderful people in my life."

"What time are you leaving tomorrow?" Beverly asked, her sunglasses hiding the sadness in her eyes.

"Around lunchtime," Ava guessed. "Everything's mostly packed. There's just some laundry left to do."

"Sounds good." Beverly rose from her chair. "Come to the beach before you go?"

"Of course!" Ava hugged her tight. "What's that expression? 'I'm not saying goodbye, just see you later.' I'll be back before you know it."

CHAPTER 34

Ava gathered the sheets and towels, still warm from the dryer and dumped them on her bed. After she folded and put them away, she would do a final sweep of the cottage and make sure everything she needed to take with her was packed. The kitchen and bathroom had already been scrubbed, the floors mopped, and the refrigerator cleaned out. Earlier in the day, she had taken a new bar of soap still in its wrapper to the outdoor shower. Smiling as she placed it on the soap dish, she had promised to be back soon.

As the hours ticked by, Ava's excitement at returning to Wicks Falls grew. She was eager to get back to work and see her friends. Casey was expecting her at The Tea Cozy first thing in the morning; they would have a lot to catch up on.

Ava was so grateful to Casey for managing things in her absence. A promotion was definitely in order for her. If Casey agreed, Ava thought sharing managerial duties would be a good thing for both of them. She had learned her lesson: don't take time for granted. Beverly had helped her to see that.

Beverly. Ava checked the hallway clock surprised to see it was already noon. She chided herself for dilly-dallying; she had to get to Halsey Pier. Sliding on her sneakers, she grabbed her sunglasses with one hand, spritzing sunscreen on her skin with the other. She slipped her house keys into her pocket and walked to the beach.

Breathing the salt air deep into her lungs, Ava was more optimistic then she had been in a long time. The future was full of possibilities. The hardest part would be facing Charlotte. Ava could still learn a lot from her if Charlotte would let her. But, Charlotte would also have to understand that Ava was her own person, with her own way of doing things. She was confident they would figure it out.

Closing in on Halsey Pier, Ava could just make out Beverly hidden behind her easel. Today, she was dressed in pale blue pants with a matching tunic, her hair pulled back in her trademark chignon. The sea breeze took hold of the fabric, swaying it to and fro. Stepping back from her work, Beverly studied a canvas perched upon the easel, the end of her paintbrush tucked in her mouth per usual. Ava wondered what it was: seagulls? A boat? A seascape? Whatever it was, Beverly was probably happy for the change of pace from Ava's emotionally taxing paintings.

"Hello there!" Ava called out. "You look very intense." She laughed as Beverly jumped at the sound of her voice.

"Ava!" Beverly called back. "Your timing is perfect." She left the easel behind her as she walked to meet Ava in the sand.

Ava greeted Beverly with good news. "I want you to know that I woke up this morning feeling better than I have in weeks, and it's all because of you. I'm finally at peace with everything. And you know what else? I had an 'aha' moment, the kind my mom used to talk about. That dark cloud I told you was always hanging over me? It was totally of my own making."

Beverly's eyes widened with surprise. "My goodness! You're like a whole new person. Now, promise me you'll *stay* happy, no more dark clouds and come back soon to Sully Shores."

"Of course, I will!" Ava laughed. "You're the reason I'll be coming back, you and this beautiful beach." She swept her arm along the horizon.

"I told you, your timing is perfect. Come see what I've been working on." Beverly grabbed Ava's hand and led her back to her easel. "This came to me yesterday. I stayed up half the night to finish it, but it still needed some last-minute touches, so I brought it to the beach for a little extra inspiration. I think it might be for you."

Ava stared at the picture. On the canvas were three figures: a man, a woman, and a small girl of about seven or eight. They were crouched together on the shore peering at a piece of brown glass in the man's cupped hands. Halsey Pier stood in the background, the sea at low tide, seagulls flying overhead.

Moving in for a closer look, Ava recognized her father, from all those years ago, the summer they had named the cottage. It had been a magical day for all three of them, and one that she would never forget. Even though her parents were no longer with her, they would always be a part of her. Finally, Ava realized what her mother had been trying to tell her all along: Life is about the connections you make; family and friends, each one there to contribute in some way to your life's journey. There are no guarantees, no promised time; it is up to each of us to make the most of every day, to cherish the people brought into our lives, and, of course, to watch for the signs. Coincidences, after all, happen for a reason.

I'm going to send you someone good.

About the Authors

Friends Leigh Brown and Victoria Corliss became co-authors in 2009. In 2013, they published their first novel, *Second Chances*. Their second book, *The Pie Sisters* was released in 2015. Their newest book, *The Pendulum's Truth*, debuted in 2018.

As active speakers and book event participants, Leigh and Victoria are often asked: 1) Are they sisters and 2) How do they write books together? They are sisters in spirit only; sisters of the heart as they like to say. To learn how their collaboration works, visit their website at http://www.browncorlissbooks.com.

They especially enjoy interacting with their readers and speaking to book clubs. Contact them at browncorlissbooks@gmail.com to make arrangements.

Paperback and e-copies of The Pendulum's Truth, The Pie Sisters, and Second Chances are available at http://amazon.com, http://barnesandnoble.com, and www.smashwords.com.